Carl Weber's:

Five Families of New York

Part 1: Brooklyn

Carl Weber's:
Five Families of New York

Part 1: Brooklyn

C. N. Phillips

www.urbanbooks.net

Urban Books, LLC
300 Farmingdale Road, N.Y.-Route 109
Farmingdale, NY 11735

Carl Weber's: Five Families of New York Part 1: Brooklyn
Copyright © 2021 C. N. Phillips

ISBN 13: 978-1-64556-119-4
ISBN 10: 1-64556-119-4

First Trade Paperback Printing April 2021
Printed in the United States of America

10 9 8 7 6 5 4 3 2 1

*This is a work of fiction. Any references or similarities
to actual events, real people, living or dead, or to real
locales are intended to give the novel a sense of reality.
Any similarity in other names, characters, places, and
incidents is entirely coincidental.*

Distributed by Kensington Publishing Corp.
Submit Orders to:
Customer Service
400 Hahn Road
Westminster, MD 21157-4627
Phone: 1-800-733-3000
Fax: 1-800-659-2436

Carl Weber's:
Five Families of New York
Part 1: Brooklyn

by

C. N. Phillips

Chapter 1

The forceful sound of a set of tall double doors opening and hitting the wall stoppers made everyone inside of a large high-rise office look up. If they had been in the middle of conversation, they were quiet as church mice when they saw the fiery eyes of the man who'd just burst in. Caesar King stood in the doorway, surveying his three peers sitting at the circular table before him. Diana, Marco, and Li all had the same question written across their faces.

"Leave." Caesar motioned for their entourages to wait outside the door with his own hired hands. "And close the door behind you."

They obliged him, and within seconds they were out of the room. As soon as they were all gone, Diana, a woman in her sixties who had aged like fine wine, leaned forward in her seat. She watched Caesar like a hawk with her light brown eyes as she awaited his next words. But she knew what those words would be. They all did. News traveled fast through the underworld grapevine. That much Caesar was certain of.

"I called you all here tonight because I want you to hear from me that it's true." Caesar's deep baritone voice vibrated off the walls. "Barry is dead. His boy still needs to identify his body, but it's him. His people phoned me when his body was found earlier in one of the drop spots they rarely use."

"Shit," Marco said, shaking his head.

"How did this happen?" Li asked in his usual fast rate of speech. "No one has dared to step out of line since the Pact was put into place."

"I don't know how, but I can tell you that it wasn't quick. These were sent to me from an unknown number." Caesar pulled his phone out and passed it around the table. "Whoever did this made sure Barry suffered. He was tortured, terribly. And they sent those to me as a warning."

"Are . . . are his toes missing?" Diana asked, aghast.

"Yes, they are," Caesar confirmed. "Along with his ears and his tongue."

"Who would do such a thing?" Li asked.

"No, the real question is, how did they get close to him in the first place?" Marco chimed in. "It had to have been an inside job."

"I don't know." Caesar gritted his teeth as he took his phone back. "But it's something that we all need to look into."

"It wasn't anybody in my camp," Diana's smooth, soft voice spoke up. "They know the consequences of breaking the Pact."

"As do those in my camp," Li said. "The Chinese know honor. There is no honor in this."

Everyone turned to Marco, who seemed to be lost in thought. When he noticed all the attention he was getting, he hurried to sit up straight. "You motherfuckers would be foolish to believe that anybody under me would be dumb enough to harm any leader of the Five Families."

"Weren't you the last to see Barry out of all of us?" Diana asked suspiciously.

"*Sí,* he came to see me. But that don't mean me or any of my people killed him, Diana."

"Why was he in Queens?" Caesar asked Marco.

"Guns. We were conducting business. I was telling him about a new shipment of military-grade weapons that just arrived, and I wanted to see if he needed a few for his men. He was supposed to come back with payment to receive them, but he never showed up. It was unlike him to do, but I figured something must have come up."

"Diana, why do you think Marco was the last to see Barry?" Caesar turned to her.

"He came to the club," Diana answered, making reference to her gentlemen's club. "You know Barry was always too bourgeoisie for the pussy I have walking the streets and was never too proud to walk through the doors of the Sugar Trap. After he relieved himself with his favorite girls, we talked for a second. It didn't hit me until now that he seemed . . . on edge."

"On edge?"

"Maybe that's not the right phrase for it. But most times after a man drains his dick, he's more relaxed than he's ever been. Barry seemed unsettled about something. I never asked what. However, he did tell me he was going to stop over in Queens to see Marco before he went home."

Caesar mulled over her words and couldn't help but wonder if what she said was true, about Barry behaving that way. He'd known Barry many years, and nowhere in his memory consisted of him outwardly showing his discomfort about any situation. It made whoever had done him in even more curious to Caesar. Who could put fear into Barry Tolliver's heart? Nobody Caesar knew, and that left him once again at a dead end.

He looked at Diana, Li, and Marco, trying to see through any lies that may have been told. But he wasn't sure they had told any. They'd all respected the Pact all those years with only minor disagreements among them.

The Pact was something put into place after they all went to war with each other. Back when they were all fighting, Caesar's father was still alive. King Cal groomed his son as his right-hand man to be the king and take over when he was gone. The fighting was always over turf, who was allowed to do what where. King Cal always told him the other Families knew that they were the strongest Family, so they would do whatever they had to do to weaken them. And they did. Many died over those notions, including Caesar's mother, who was killed in cold blood. Caesar never found out which Family was responsible for shooting her through the window of her Cadillac at a traffic light. But that was the moment that forever changed his fate.

When Caesar was 12, his father, the kingpin of Manhattan, had already started grooming him to take over the game. By 14, Caesar had already taken his first life. It didn't stop there. He had so much rage inside of him from his mother's murder that he jumped headfirst into the war. He had been just a kid, but Caesar was respected and feared all over New York. He was a menace. But when his father died in 1978, Caesar called for a ceasefire. It took him losing too soon the last parent he had to realize how much senseless violence had taken place among the Five Families over one thing: money. The other Families respected the King Cal legacy enough to stop fighting and listen to Caesar's proposal.

Each Family was given a trade. The Colombians were given the prostitution game in Harlem. The Mexicans were given a weapons operation in Queens. The Asians were loan sharks who loaned both money and hired hands at a cost in the Bronx. The other black Family ran their own theft ring in Brooklyn while Caesar remained the kingpin in Manhattan. Under the Pact, every Family was off-limits to another, and due to the difference in trades, business could be conducted in each other's territories. They would be allies and always aid each other in need. At the end of each month, each Family would have to pay their dues into the pot. That money went toward, but not limited to, community action, cleaning up their messes, and the occasional payoff to the police department.

Somehow, they all agreed. And there they were decades later still living in peace. Or so they thought. If none of them broke the Pact, someone did. And that was what they needed to find out.

"Until we know who did this, I need everyone in this room to tighten up on security. Nobody, and I mean nobody"—Caesar cut his eyes to Diana—"is to go anywhere alone."

"Don't look at me like that," Diana said snippily. "I can handle myself."

"You may look good for your age, but that doesn't change the fact that you're sixty-four. Keep someone with you at least until I have a conversation with the Italians."

The Italians were the only ones who did not sign the Pact. Their territory was in Staten Island, and they did a little bit of everything. However, since they didn't sign, they weren't permitted to do business anywhere else. Knowing about the alliance, they never tried anything foolish, seeing that they would have the weight of the Five Families on their back. Still, Caesar figured it would do good to pay his old friend Bosco a visit.

"This might not be the right time to say this," Marco said, clearing his throat, "but who's gonna fill that seat?" He nodded toward Barry's empty seat.

He was right. It wasn't the right time. However, it was something that had to be talked about. Another clause in the Pact was that no head chair would be left empty if someone stepped down or died. However, not just anyone could be a replacement. There had to be a vote.

"It's tradition to pass the family business down to the oldest child," Diana reminded him, and Caesar raised a brow.

"His boy is only twentysomething." Caesar shook his head.

"And isn't he in school to be a chef?" Li spat and shook his head. "Barry didn't even mold him to take over anything. What about his friend? He seems to have good leadership skills."

"Julius? He's too power hungry." Diana shook her head. "Giving him a seat would be the wrong move. Sometimes there is a reason for a second in command. I say we give the boy a chance. Caesar, you may think he's young, but you were around the same age he is now when you formed the Pact. Even younger when you got into this business. I've been around the kid a time or two. He's a bright kid. Real smart."

"But what does he know about the underworld?" Marco threw in, trying to thwart the idea. "The kid is trying to be a chef for crying out loud. If Barry wanted him to know the family business, he would have already been groomed."

"How do we know he isn't and just chose a different path?" Li pondered.

"I don't know," Caesar sighed. "But we have to vote on it."

"I say hell no," Marco spoke up.

"Well, I say we wait on the vote," Diana said.

"Wait for what?" he asked.

"For Caesar to check the kid out and bring him before us." Diana and Caesar connected eyes.

"Diana . . ." He started.

"Barry only had one child. It would be disrespectful to his family name to vote his legacy to someone who didn't build it," she said, and it was her turn to cut her eyes at him.

If Caesar was the godfather of the Families, Diana was the godmother. They'd grown close over the years and had always been able to give each other counsel when needed. Caesar sighed again and nodded reluctantly. He hated to admit it, but she was right.

"All right. Julius will fill in for the time being since business must continue and dues must be paid. In the meantime, I'll check the kid out. But as of right now, Barry's seat is vacant."

Chapter 2

Breathing heavily, Bryshon "Boogie" Tolliver fell through the door of his Brooklyn condo in a rush. He checked the hallway behind him to make sure he had not been followed before shutting the door. Stumbling into the large kitchen area, he let the loaded duffle bag on his shoulder fall to the ground and gripped the edge of a counter tightly with his hands. Beads of sweat dripped off the tip of his nose as he thought about how everything that night had gone wrong. His eyes fell on the slightly open duffle bag at his feet. A few stacks of hundreds were poking out. It barely seemed worth it at that moment.

Growing up on fast money, Boogie was used to a more upscale lifestyle. He had grown accustomed to designer clothes, fast cars, and fine places to live. All of that just added value to his good looks and charming smile. However, when he decided that he wanted to follow his dream of becoming a chef, his father, Barry Tolliver, cut him off for not following in his footsteps in the family business. Boogie was able to keep his Ferrari and his condo, but his line to the family account had been snipped. And because of that, he had to figure out a way to make money on his own.

Boogie was 12 when Barry began teaching him how to be the perfect crook. Not only did he learn how to use a gun, but he learned how to pick every kind of lock and open any kind of safe. In fact, he grew a knack for it, so much that he figured he could make a side job out of it to keep some paper in his pockets while attending New York University. Finding and hitting licks wasn't hard, given the fact that his rich college peers were so chatty. They had no discretion when letting it be known that their folks would be out of town for the weekend or when inviting anybody and everybody over for the kind of wild college parties where everyone ended up passed out drunk. That was Boogie's favorite kind of lick because they were so easy. Not only that, but he always left with cash. He never tried to leave anyone's home with their assets, because in order to get them gone he would have to contact Toby, Barry's fence. Toby would buy almost anything and could sell it without a trace. However, he still worked for Barry, which meant that was where his loyalty rested. Toby eventually told Barry what Boogie had been doing, which led to Barry making a surprise visit to Boogie's home the night after finals.

"I knew this shit was in your blood, boy," Barry had told him. "How about I cut you a deal?"

"What kind of deal?"

"Work with me in the summer and part-time while you're in school. Give the family business a real go. None of this petty shit you've been doing, but some real hard-hitter shit. You'll even have your own team."

"And if I still don't want that life forever?"

"Then I let you be Chef Boogie in peace," Barry said with a shrug.

"You're serious?"

"I already cut your access to the family account back on," Barry told him and gave him a look of sincerity. "Look, son, you know I'm not good at this heart-to-heart shit, but you're my only boy. And this time without you around hasn't been easy on me. I admit that I might have been a little harsh by doing away with you so easily. You're your own man, and in order to not lose you, I have to accept that."

"Okay," Boogie said after a few moments of thinking over his father's proposal. "We can get busy this summer, but when school starts back up, I'm out."

"We'll see."

The truth was that Boogie had been serious about wanting to get out of the game. After he graduated college, he planned on moving to the West Coast and opening his own restaurant along Santa Monica Beach. With school starting back up soon, he was trying to find the right time to tell his father the news. However, now he didn't know if he would even make it that far. He'd messed up, bad. And he didn't think even Barry could get him out of that one, especially since the job he'd gone on had been off the record.

The team Boogie had been working with that summer was a solid one. It consisted of three other men besides Boogie. A-Rod, Bentley, and Kirk were thorough, and the heists they went on together went off without a hitch. The only thing was that, as a collective, they were only able to keep 20 percent of their earnings while the rest went to Barry. Barry called it the operations fee, being that they were only hired hands. Soon, though, a 20 percent split per job wasn't satisfactory to the other men, and they began working jobs Barry had no idea about. If he ever found out about them, they would all be dead men, especially since the jobs could easily be tied back to him. The hits Barry sent them on were calculated, not rogue. So, when Boogie, who was supposed to be their team leader, found out, he was plagued with the decision of whether to turn them in to his father. A-Rod was a smooth talker though. He could hustle a hustler out of all his dope without ever paying a dime if he wanted to. And Boogie fell for it. Although, thinking back, he wished he hadn't.

"C'mon, man. Your pops will never find out about this. We get in and we get out. Simple."

Boogie listened to the words coming out of A-Rod's mouth, coupled with the sure expression on his face, and still felt unsure of what was being put on the table. He glanced at Kirk and Bentley, taking notice that they were watching him like a hawk at their table. The four men had met up at a local diner for what had seemed like a casual lunch, but in truth Boogie had just wanted to tell them that he'd found out about the jobs they were doing on the side. The streets were talking, and soon the wind would carry those whispers to Barry. Somehow the conversation had gone from telling them to get back on track, to A-Rod trying to talk Boogie into joining them on one last off-the-record hit.

"So, you in or out?" A-Rod prodded at Boogie's silence. "Two hundred thousand dollars split four ways, man. Think about all that money."

Boogie knew he should say no. He knew he should put his foot down and take charge right then and there. "I don't know, man," Boogie sighed.

"Of course you don't," A-Rod scoffed. "A little fifty thousand ain't shit to a rich nigga like you. You rollin' in your daddy's dough, ain't you?"

"Yo, you buggin'. I make my own money, you know that."

"Prove it," A-Rod said, and beside them the other two men smirked. "Pop out with us this one last time. Let's get this money, and then we go back to doing whatever Barry asks us to. You down?"

In truth, Boogie didn't know why he didn't get up and leave right then. He didn't have anything to prove to them, but still he didn't like for anybody to test him. He pushed his better judgment to the side and nodded his head.

"*One last job, and then no more shit off the record, understand?*"

"*Loud and clear.*" A-Rod nodded.

"*Do you even have the details on this hit? Or are you just going for the home because of how it looks?*"

"*Now, nigga, do you think I would hit a house and just assume there were two hundred racks inside?*"

"*I would hope not.*"

"*Well, I wouldn't. I've done my research, and I know a condo at the Beau is a drop spot.*"

"*Whose drop spot?*"

"*Some nobody-ass hustlers.*" A-Rod shrugged. Bentley nodded his head. Kirk reserved a blank expression on his face while A-Rod spoke. "*Just some niggas tryin'a get their operation off the ground.*"

"*Caesar's people are the only ones who deal in these parts,*" Boogie said with a raised brow. "*I ain't robbing Caesar. That shit is against law.*"

"*That's the thing. They ain't Caesar's people,*" A-Rod told him, shaking his head. "*They've been moving weight all over New York under the radar. The way I see it, we'll be doing Caesar a big favor by taking all that paper off them boys' hands.*"

To that Boogie had to laugh, and the others joined in. "*You a foo', boy. But a'ight, what's the plan?*"

"*I done had Bentley watching these niggas for the past few weeks. Tell him what you saw, G.*"

Bentley, a soft-spoken young man, leaned in to the table. Boogie glanced over his shoulder to make sure nobody was paying them any mind. When he was sure nobody was focused on them, he too leaned in to the table to listen with the rest.

"*These are young niggas we're dealin' with,*" Bentley started in a low voice.

"*Boy, we're young niggas,*" Kirk commented.

"Nah, they ain't built like us. We're more thorough. These niggas must have just gotten in the game. Everything every day is done on the same schedule. Way too easy to clock. Mondays they get their shipment from a van with California plates, dropped off at the old Clenton laundromat over in Bed-Stuy. Tuesdays through Thursday they hit the block. Hard. Because by Friday, they're making their cash drop-offs to the condo at seven thirty on the dot. But by Saturday, all the money is moved."

"You seen them move it?"

"I mean, I assume that's what's in those briefcases being loaded into that same black van."

"So how do you know there will be two hundred thousand dollars there?" Boogie inquired.

"Truthfully, I just aimed low." Bentley shrugged. "I really think there is more though. Mainly because everybody knows Caesar got the drug game on lock here. Even outsiders. I don't think these niggas are trying to take over the territory. I think they're tryin'a get in and get out while demand is high and the market is hot."

"So, in short, they're making that paper," Kirk said.

"And I want all of it," A-Rod said.

"How do we get inside?" Boogie said, now just as eager as the rest. "If they're holding that kind of paper, it's gon' be guarded. And they ain't gon' just let us walk up to the door."

"We got that covered," Bentley said with a twinkle in his eyes. "At eight o'clock every night the condo's cleaning service makes their rounds around the building collecting laundry of tenants. That's thirty minutes after the drop-off. I bet the money won't even be out of the bags yet."

"You got all this by watching from outside?"

"Nah, nigga. I got all this from the condo's website," Bentley answered. "The place is fancy as shit. They have a restaurant and all that. I also sneaked one of the employee work uniforms earlier this week. It's big enough to fit one of us."

"Nigga, how the fuck did you pull that off?" Kirk asked, clearly impressed.

"The bitch working the front desk was a dud. She was mesmerized by all this chocolate, and she thought I was one of 'Mr. Shane's guests.' She even gave me the room number and buzzed me up. I ain't get too close, but it's for sure our room. I could tell by the two big niggas standing outside the door. So, you right about one thing, Boog. But even niggas that big can't stop a bullet."

"Wait," Boogie said, making a sudden realization. "Tomorrow's Friday. Y'all tryin'a hit this lick tomorrow?"

"Is that a problem?"

"Nah," Boogie's mouth said, but his mind spoke the complete opposite.

"A'ight then, I guess all we need to figure out is who's playin' dress-up," A-Rod said.

"Man, I can't believe y'all got me in this stupid-ass fit," Kirk grumbled and pulled the collar of his shirt. His trimmed hair was neatly lined, and he wore the green and white stolen employee work attire. He looked like a square, but that was what he was going for. They were all in a stolen unmarked vehicle that had tinted windows, with A-Rod as the driver.

"Just get in there and do what you're here to do," Bentley told him.

"Yeah, yeah. Next time it's gon' be you dressed as a flop."

It was twenty minutes until eight, and they had just pulled down the street from the tall condominium. When the car stopped, Kirk got out of the back seat and walked the rest of the way to the front doors of the condo while they parked and waited for his text. He was to walk in like a regular employee and prop the back-alley entrance open as well as adjust any camera views back there.

Boogie, Bentley, and A-Rod screwed the silencers on their guns while they waited. Dressed in all black, Boogie was happy to see that the sun had started to set. That meant they would be shielded by the shadows as they ran in and out. Boogie was prepared to do what he had to do, but just like any other time, he hoped he wouldn't have to. Yet he had an uneasy feeling in his gut. He'd never gone on a job after only knowing about it for a day. He viewed all of his licks as miniature heists: they needed to be well thought out before they could be executed. But he had to give it to his crew. They had done their research, and he knew firsthand how on point they were. He pushed the uneasy feeling to the back of his mind when he heard Bentley's phone vibrate.

"We're clear," he told A-Rod, who pulled away from the curb. "He said to take the back way to the stairs."

When they were parked in the empty back alley, out of the cameras' sights, they moved quickly. They pulled their bandana masks over their faces and each grabbed a duffle bag before hopping out of the car. The heavy metal door to the building had been propped open with a phone book, which Boogie kicked out of the way when they went through. Boogie was in front while A-Rod covered their backs. The cold air instantly hit the part of Boogie's face that wasn't covered, and the aroma of food being cooked seeped through the mask. They must have been near the kitchen. The hallway they were in was brightly lit, which meant they would have to get to where they were going quick and try to avoid any cameras. They found the staircase Kirk had told them about and hurried up it, pistols drawn.

"Floor five," Bentley told them as they traveled upstairs. "It's eight o'clock on the dot. Kirk should be in place right now."

Upon reaching floor five, Boogie peered through the small square window into the hall. Sure enough, his eyes fell on Kirk, who had a laundry cart in tow. He was standing outside a door talking to two big men. One had a darker complexion, and the other was the color of peanut butter. Their backs were to the door at the end of the hall, but Boogie gave Kirk a small nod when their eyes met briefly. It seemed that there was a nasty exchange going on, and the men looked angry. Quietly, Boogie opened the door slightly so that he, A-Rod, and Bentley could slip through.

"Shane told that bitch downstairs that there was no need to send one of you motherfuckas to this door again. We can wash our own fuckin' clothes. Understand?" the darker of the two men was saying.

"I apologize about that, sir," Kirk told them. "I'm new. I didn't know that."

"Well, take your new ass away from this door," the other man said, pushing Kirk in the chest, forcing him to step back. "If I ever see you by this door again, I'ma break your ugly face. Go find a real job. You should be embarrassed."

"Fam, they got this nigga lookin' like a li'l leprechaun and shit," the dark-skinned man said, and they both laughed.

The sound of guns cocking silenced their joy.

"Well, then I guess that means his pot of gold is on the other side of that door then, huh?" Boogie said, placing

his weapon against the temple of the dark-skinned guard.

"Ah, ah!" A-Rod said to the other when he went for his gun. "I'll lay your pit bull–lookin' ass down if you try that. Don't think about tryin'a yell either, 'cause that ain't gon' do shit but give your mama a closed casket."

He grabbed the gun from the man's waist, and Boogie did the same to his captive. They tossed both weapons into the laundry basket beside them. Kirk became the lookout, and Bentley's weapon went from one man to the other.

"What's your name?" A-Rod asked the man he was holding. When the man didn't say anything, A-Rod placed the tip of the silencer between his eyes. "I asked a question."

"Trent," the man finally said.

"Well, Trent, I need you to tell me a few things. And if I find out you're lying, you know what's gon' happen. How many people are behind this door?"

"Just one. Everybody else just left."

"Just one, huh?"

"Yeah, man. Just Shane."

"Good. Knock."

A-Rod pushed Trent's face toward the peephole and forced him to knock on the door. It took a few moments, but soon they could hear footsteps coming toward the door. There was a loud sound of lips smacking when the footsteps reached the door. It swung open and revealed a light-skinned man sporting messy braids, wearing nothing but a pair of basketball shorts and a pair of socks.

"Man, Trent, what the fuck you want? I was about to start the coun—"

His statement was cut short when A-Rod hit Trent in the back of the head so hard he passed out. His body fell into Shane's, and the rest of them filed into the condo.

"Dune, what the fuck is goin' on?" Shane asked, sounding like he was from the West Coast. He threw his hands up as he stared at three guns pointed his way.

Boogie assumed Dune was the man he'd just shoved to the marble floor of the luxurious condo. The front door led right into the kitchen, and judging by the lines of cocaine on the dining room table, Shane was about to get into a little more than just counts. The next thing Boogie spotted was the large pile of banded stacks on a table in the living room straight ahead.

"Four, keep one on him," Boogie said, instructing Kirk to put his burner on Dune. They never used each other's real names on a job. Boogie then focused his attention on Shane while A-Rod and Bentley cased the rest of the home, just in case Trent had been lying. When they came back into the kitchen, they nodded at Boogie, letting him know the coast was clear.

"Yo, who the fuck are you niggas? And do you know who the fuck I am?"

"We some niggas who don't give a fuck about who you are," A-Rod spat and shoved Shane's head with his gun. "All we care about is that paper over there. Three, go load that shit up!" He and Boogie tossed Bentley their bags so that he could start putting money in them.

Shane chuckled as he shook his head. "Y'all don't know what you're getting yourselves into, man. Walk out of here with that money and you'll have a target on your back for the rest of your lives. What's left of them anyways."

"Is that s'posed to scare us, nigga?" Boogie asked, almost amused. "Y'all the ones dealin' in a territory everybody knows is off-limits."

"Y'all Caesar's people?" Shane asked almost timidly, and at that Boogie did chuckle.

"Nah, if we were Caesar's people, you would be dead already," he said. "So, consider this your lucky day. 'Cause all we're gon' take is the money, and we won't even say shit about the little operation you've been runnin' under his nose."

"Hurry up, Three!"

"I'm tryin, but this is a lot of fuckin' money!" Bentley called.

He had already filled up two bags and was working on the third. Things were going smoothly, but Boogie was ready to get out of there. They were all so busy watching Dune and Shane and making sure they didn't try anything funny that they had forgotten about Trent passed out by the front door. It wasn't until Boogie noticed Shane's eyes looking at something behind him that he realized they had messed up.

Boogie whipped his head around just in time to see a not-so-knocked-out Trent snatch a gun that was strapped to the bottom of the dining room table. He aimed it at the person closest to him.

"Four!" Boogie shouted, but he wasn't fast enough.

Trent fingered his trigger, and the loud boom from the gun got everybody's attention. Kirk didn't even see coming the bullet that hit him right in the dome. When he dropped to the floor dead, Dune grabbed the pistol in his hand and started firing wild shots at the rest of them. Boogie jumped out of the way just in time, but A-Rod was caught in his chest. However, that wasn't before he let off a few rounds himself. Shane took A-Rod's bullets to the face before falling to the ground.

"Boss!" Dune shouted and tried to get to Shane.

Boogie had something for him, though. He tugged at his trigger, lighting Dune's body up before he could take one step. He was dead before he hit the marble. Boogie's reaction to Trent coming up on him was too slow, and he was a sitting duck.

Pfft! Pfft! Pfft!

Boogie felt bullets whizzing by his face and saw three red circles appear in the middle of Trent's wide chest. The look of shock on his face when he realized he'd been hit was priceless. In a daze, Boogie turned around and saw Bentley standing there with his gun pointed and all three bags of money on his shoulder.

"C'mon, Boogie, we gotta go!" Bentley shouted and went over to A-Rod's body to get the car keys from his pocket. "Nigga, come on!"

Boogie snapped out of it and hurried to his feet. He took the duffle bag from Bentley, and the two of them rushed out of the condo. There were people poking their heads out of their doors due to hearing the multiple gunshots. Some gasped as they ran past them, and Boogie saw a few with their phones to their ears, calling the police, he was sure. In a place like that, he was positive, the response time was lightning fast, so the best thing they could do was shake the spot as quickly as possible.

They exited the way they came and took the stairs three at a time on the way down. Once they were outside and in the car, Bentley backed into the street and sped off. He made to pull his mask down, but Boogie stopped him.

"Nah, not until we're off these streets and at the warehouse," Boogie said, pointing at all the buildings surrounding them. "Cameras."

Bentley nodded his head in understanding but didn't say anything. They rode in silence all the way back to the abandoned warehouse they'd all met at earlier that day. When the car slowed to a stop under a flickering streetlight, Bentley turned the car off, and they finally *removed their face masks. Neither man spoke. The only sound that could be heard were the crickets in the distance.*

"Fuck!" Bentley suddenly shouted and hit the steering wheel so hard the car shook. "That shit was not s'posed to go down like that. Them niggas . . . them niggas dead, yo."

"I knew we shouldn't have gone on this fuckin' job," Boogie said, shaking his head. "Now what the fuck we gon' tell my pops?"

"I don't know," Bentley answered. "But what I do know is that we need to get rid of this car and get the fuck out of here."

He was right. Boogie grabbed the bags of money while Bentley went to the trunk and got a can of gasoline from it. He doused the entire car with it and tossed a match inside. Boogie stood back and watched the flames grow and dance with the small gusts of wind.

"That should be good," Bentley said and picked up two bags. "I think I got a little more than you. Take some stacks. There gotta be at least half a mil here."

He started to open one of the bags and give Boogie some of the money, which was originally supposed to be split four ways, but Boogie shook his head. He didn't need it. "You keep it," Boogie said. "You might need it after my dad finds out about what happened tonight. I don't even think I'ma be safe from his wrath."

Bentley nodded his head and threw up two fingers in farewell. He started jogging up the street toward wherever his car was parked, and Boogie went the other way.

Snapping out of his memory, Boogie wiped the sweat from his forehead. The streets would be talking by the morning. He knew he'd better prepare for that phone call.

Bzzz! Bzzz!

He almost jumped when he felt his phone vibrate in his pants pocket. Did his dad already know what happened? He was afraid to look at the caller ID, but when he did, he saw a number that wasn't saved in his phone.

"Bryshon?" a voice he didn't recognize said on the other end.

"Who is this?" Boogie inquired.

"It's Caesar."

"Cae . . . uh, do you have the right number?" Boogie tried to even his voice. "Were you tryin'a reach my pops or somethin'?" Did he know what had happened? And how had he gotten his number? So many questions were going through Boogie's head that he almost didn't hear what Caesar said next.

"No, son. I'm calling about your father. You need to come down to the police station."

"The police station? Did my pops get bumped up?"

"No, Bryshon. Your father is dead."

Chapter 3

Boogie had never felt a numbness like the one he felt at that very moment. It was the next morning, and he was at the police station. He was standing there in front of a table with a stranger, waiting for another stranger to pull the white sheet back. Barry had taught him that a man was supposed to hold his emotions in and always keep his composure. But when Boogie saw the very same man who had taught him that lying there with a chunk of his face missing, he couldn't do anything. His body screamed while his soul cried, but his mind was just reminding him to keep breathing.

"That's . . . that's him. That's my pops," he finally was able to say breathily to the officers standing close by.

"Thank you," one of them said. "We'll give you some time."

When the cops and mortician were gone, Boogie's hand grabbed Barry's cold one and gripped it tightly. "Who did this to you, man?"

"That's what I'm going to find out," a voice sounded beside him.

Boogie blinked away his tears before turning his head to face the one and only Caesar King. They were both tall men, but Caesar had him by an inch or two. Boogie noticed of his clenched jaw and the serious expression on his face.

"I thought the heads of the Five Families were off-limits," Boogie said, unable to control his glare.

"I did too, son. I did too. Someone broke the Pact. And I won't rest until I figure out who. Because this wasn't just a murder. It was a message."

"A message for who? You?"

"For all of us. Why? I don't know. The only thing I know right now is that Barry's seat at the table is empty and—"

"My pops hasn't even been on ice for a day, and you're already tryin'a get me to take his spot?" Boogie asked, letting his dad's hand go. "I still have to tell my mother that the reason her husband didn't come home last night is the same reason he'll never come home again! I ain't thinkin' 'bout no fuckin' seat at a table."

He turned to walk away, but Caesar's voice stopped him.

"I didn't say anything about wanting you to take Barry's seat. Your father spent most of his life building the empire you've known your whole life. He wouldn't want it to go to anybody else. Go tell your mother what you need to tell her, and get in touch with me by the end of the week, you hear?"

Boogie wanted to tell him to go straight to hell, but even in his anger he knew Caesar wasn't the one to take it out on. He'd only been around him a handful of times growing up, but he knew that the streets didn't speak loudly on Caesar's name. They whispered enough stories about him for Boogie to know that he was the real-life boogeyman. So instead he just nodded and left the room.

He couldn't even feel his feet touching the floor. The entire ride to the police station he'd been hoping, praying, that somebody had gotten it wrong, that it wouldn't be his father under that sheet. But his worst fears had been confirmed. He had never even entertained the idea of what he would do without Barry, mainly because he just always thought he would have more time with him. His mother was going to be devastated. She and Barry .. been together way before Boogie was even thought of.

When he got into his car and drove to the home he'd grown up in, he contemplated how he would break the news to her. But by the time he pulled into the circular driveway of the mansion, he had come up with nothing. He sighed and shook his head before he got out of the car. As he walked up to the home, the doors flung open, and there his mother, Dina Tolliver, was in her normal designer suit getup. The only thing different she wore was a face full of tears. By the expression on her face, Boogie could tell that she already knew. Before he could ask how, she spoke.

"I . . . I just got off the phone with an officer. Please tell me what he's saying isn't real. Did you . . . did you just identify Barry's body?"

He wished that he could tell her it was a lie, a prank even. But he couldn't. And facing her, he also realized that he couldn't tell her it was the truth. Still, all she had to do was look at his puffy eyes and exhausted demeanor to figure out the answer. Boogie moved fast enough to catch her as her legs gave out. She began to sob uncontrollably, and the sight broke his heart.

"C'mon, Mama, let's get you in the house."

She shook in his arms as he helped her stand, and the two went back inside. They went and sat in the sitting room, the one no kids were allowed in when he was growing up. Boogie held her and let her cry into his shoulder. He even shed a few more tears himself.

Everything in their home reminded him of Barry, from the chandelier that hung from the tall ceiling to the tile floors. Barry had the original light fixtures replaced because of the way the moonlight shone through tall windows in the sitting room. He said he wanted a crystal chandelier in there so that when he danced with his wife at home, it would be as if they were at a fancy ball. The tile on the floor had replaced the carpet, but that reasoning was not so romantic. Barry had replaced all the carpet in the house, except in the bedrooms. He said if he ever had to murder someone in his home, cleaning the blood from the carpet would be too much of a hassle.

Boogie's eyes ran across all the family photos along the walls, and he recalled when most of them were taken. His attention fell on one in particular: he was about 8 years old at his first baseball game. By the way Barry was smiling in the photo, one would have assumed Boogie's team had won that day. They would have been wrong. Boogie recalled his team losing, badly. But Barry told him to keep his head held high because the taste of a loss was important to experience. He said it would teach him the value of knowing where he wanted to be: on top.

Boogie blinked his tears away again and vowed that the next tears shed over the situation would come from the eyes of whoever had killed his father. He lifted his mother's face by her chin and wiped the tears away from her face. He'd never seen her looks so defeated in his life. It was then that he knew he had to be strong for the both of them.

"I'm sorry, son," she said weakly. "I know we all die someday, but I didn't prepare for this pain to come so soon."

"Don't apologize," he told her. "Feel what you gotta feel. Just know that I'm gon' find who did this to Pops and make them pay. Do you know if anybody had beef with him over anything, Ma? I mean, did he talk about anything goin' on recently?"

"No." She shook her head in between her sniffles. "Nothing. But then again, he'd been gone so much lately we barely got the chance to do any talking. I just figured he was busy doing the things he does best. If you had told me that today would be the day I started planning my husband's funeral, I—"

"Wouldn't have believed it?" Boogie finished her sentence. "Yeah, me either. Pops was untouchable."

"Apparently not," Dina said and then grew quiet.

"Mama, how about I go make you a cup of tea? Some of that chamomile that you like?"

"That would be good, son. Thank you."

Before he left, he grabbed the white blanket his grandmother had knitted from the love seat on the other side of the room. Grandma Tolliver had knitted it for Dina when she found out she would be having a grandson. It was supposed to keep Dina's body wrapped in love while she carried her child. Boogie thought that she could use some of that love in that moment. He placed the blanket gently over her body and planted a kiss on her forehead before going to the kitchen.

The aroma of brewed coffee hit his nostrils, and he shook his head. The last thing she needed was something to give her the jitters when she had a broken heart. Boogie walked past the tall stainless-steel refrigerator to the counter where the coffee maker was. The pot was still steaming, and he figured she must have just made the coffee when she'd gotten the call, because it didn't look like even a cup had been poured. Boogie dumped its contents out into the sink before cleaning it and putting it in the dish rack. He knew how much his mother hated having dishes in the sink, even if it was just one.

After he got the tea kettle down from the hanging rack over the sink and pulled a packet of tea from one of the distressed cabinets, he started the water on the stove. He was staring at the kettle in a trance when his phone began to ring in his pocket. "Hello?" he answered solemnly.

"I just heard about what happened. You a'ight over there, nigga?" Bentley's voice came through the line.

"Nah," Boogie answered and leaned back to peek in at Dina. She was sitting on the couch, staring into space and not paying him any mind. "I ain't gon' be good until I find out who did this to him."

"I feel you on that. Damn," Bentley sighed into the phone. "I never thought anyone could touch Barry."

"You and me both."

"Ay, man," Bentley's voice grew serious. "I hate to do this to you at a time like this, but we need to meet up. Like now. To talk about one of the bitches from last night."

"Which one?" Boogie asked, catching his drift.

"The one whose house it was. Turns out she wasn't 'sleep after all while her friends partook in all the action. She moving around Brooklyn right now."

In all the commotion, Boogie had almost forgotten about the bloody escapade he and Bentley had gone on the night before, partly because he thought everyone besides him and Boogie had died, and even more so because Barry wasn't alive to be angry at them anymore. But if what Bentley was saying was true, Shane wasn't dead.

"How you know it's her?" Boogie asked, continuing to talk in code.

"I saw her with my own two eyes, laid up in a bed surrounded by niggas."

"She talkin'?"

"I don't know yet. But this ain't good."

"Fuck," Boogie cursed. "A'ight. I'll meet you at yo' spot in an hour."

"Yup."

Bentley disconnected the call, and Boogie hurried to pour the hot tea into a mug for his mother. He brought it to her and set it on a coaster on the glass coffee table in front of the couch she was on.

"Here, Mama. It's hot, so be careful," he warned. "I have to make a run, but I will try to come back later tonight."

"You're leaving me?" Her voice broke when she spoke, and it took all of Boogie's strength not to sit back down with her.

"Yeah, I gotta go handle some business. If I don't come back tonight, I'll be back tomorrow. I promise. I'll call Grandma to come sit with you today."

"Okay, son," Dina accepted sadly. "I will just see you later."

"I love you."

"I love you too, baby," she responded and pulled him into a tight embrace.

When he pulled away from her, Boogie had to avert his eyes. He knew that one more look at his mother in such a broken-down state would make him stay there with her all day. But he couldn't. That was what Grandma Tolliver was for. He made the call to her on the way out the door, but it came to light that she was already on her way to the house. She lived in New York, but she was about an hour away. Still, Boogie was comforted by the fact that she would be there soon.

He got into his car and tried not to let what Bentley had just told him completely crowd his mind. Even if Shane was still alive, there was no way he could know who had hit him up the night before. Also, he was bold for moving around the city, talking about getting robbed in Caesar's territory, a territory he wasn't even supposed to be in in the first place. Boogie rode in silence the entire drive to Bentley's apartment, also in Brooklyn.

When he arrived at the slightly tattered building, Boogie parked in visitor parking and got out of the car. He looked around and saw a young woman pushing a stroller to the front door of the building he was going to.

He hurried to catch up to her, seeing that she also had a few bags of groceries.

"Don't touch that door," he said from behind her. "I got it."

He grabbed the handle and pulled the door open so she could push her baby through. It was when she passed him to go inside that he became aware of how pretty she was. She had a smooth brown complexion and long, straight hair that went down her back. Her brown eyes were lighter than her skin, and her lips were plump and shaped like a heart. Boogie glanced at the sleeping baby girl and smiled because she was just as pretty as her mama. When he looked back up at the woman, he noticed that she was smiling too. She was so pretty that when he stepped inside, he almost didn't notice the faint smell of urine coming from down the hallway.

"Thank you," she said.

"No problem," he told her and pointed at the two seem- ingly heavy bags in her hand. "You need help with those?"

"No, it's okay. You don't have to." She shook her head. "I have to go to the third floor, and I would feel bad. I can carry my own groceries."

"Well, I guess I'll carry her then." Boogie pointed to the stroller. "I'm goin' to the third floor too, and I wouldn't feel right watchin' you struggle with all this stuff you have to carry."

She eyeballed Boogie, and he could see her contem- plating her choices in her head. He had told the truth. He did have to go to the third floor. He didn't know how high Bentley had been when he agreed to move to the third floor of a building that had no elevator.

"Okay," she finally said.

"A'ight, coo'," Boogie said and made to grab the stroller, but she pushed the groceries his way.

"I got my baby. You can carry these," she said and picked the stroller up like she'd done it a thousand times.

He knew it was probably heavy, but he didn't fight her for it. The two walked up the stairs quickly side by side. He couldn't help sneaking peeks at her and found himself grinning at the way she was huffing and puffing holding that stroller. He could tell that she was trying hard not to wake her sleeping baby.

"And what's so funny?" she asked breathlessly.

"You." Boogie grinned. "You shoulda let me carry that. You gon' blow yo' back out."

"Nigga, I do not know you for you to be carrying my daughter up some stairs," she said, shooting him an annoyed look.

"You're right," Boogie agreed. "My name is Boogie. What about you?"

"Roz," she answered. "What kinda name is Boogie, anyway?"

"A nickname," Boogie answered with a smirk. "What kinda name is Roz?"

"It's short for Rosaline," she said.

"And her name?" Boogie nodded to the baby, and Roz hesitated.

"Amber," she finally answered. "She's one."

"Amber. I like that."

When they finally reached the third floor, Roz placed the stroller on the ground and tried to catch her breath. Boogie gestured down the hallway toward all the doors on either side. Bentley's apartment was at the end of the hall, but he figured he could drop them off at their door first. "Lead the way," he said.

"Ooh wee, I didn't know I was this out of shape," she said and started down the hall. "That trip just almost took me out!"

"Don't you take that trip every day if you live here?" Boogie asked, and Roz laughed.

"I don't live here. I'm just here bringing my brother some things for his place."

"Brother?" Boogie inquired.

His question was answered when she led him all the way down to Bentley's unit. When they got there, she turned to him and smiled.

"Thank you for everything, but this is where I have to tell you to skate. My brother has a real mean streak when it comes to seeing me with niggas. Especially after what Amber's dad did to me. I don't even want those problems."

"Me either." Boogie smirked, reaching over her shoulder and knocking on the door.

"Who is it?" Bentley's voice barked.

"It's me, nigga," Boogie said and watched the shock spread on Roz's face when the door opened.

She whipped to face Bentley, who seemed surprised to see the three of them at his doorstep. He glanced behind them before stepping back and letting them into his home. When he shut the door, he locked it and turned to his sister. "Roz, what you doin' here?"

"Didn't you ask me to get you some food for your fridge?" she asked and pointed at the bags in Boogie's hands.

"Yeah, but why is Boogie holdin' 'em? Y'all come together or somethin'?" He eyed Roz and Boogie suspiciously.

"Nah, I just met her downstairs," Boogie told him. "She had a lot of shit in her hands, so I just helped out. I didn't even know we were comin' to the same place. Why didn't you ever tell me that you had a sister?"

"It never came up," Bentley grunted and turned to Roz. "I didn't think you were gon' come until later today, sis. I got some business to handle."

"Boy, I just carried this damn stroller up three flights of stairs. You ain't kicking me out. Move."

She took the groceries from Boogie and pushed past Bentley to go to the kitchen. She ignored them like they weren't there as she started putting the contents in the bags away. Bentley watched her bustle around for a moment before he sighed and rubbed the top of his head with his hand.

"She act like my damn mama," Bentley said and looked at Boogie. "You let my sister carry this stroller up all them stairs?"

"She wouldn't let me." Boogie shrugged and looked down at Amber, who was now wide awake. "But then again I wouldn't either if I were her. Her motherly instinct probably kicked in. She ain't know me from a can of paint."

"I feel it," Bentley said, unbuckling Amber from her seat. He started making baby noises and kissing his niece's cheeks. "'Cause we all love the Burr baby, don't we? Uncle would go crazy if anything ever happened to you. With yo' pretty self. Yeah, Uncle's baby is the prettiest!"

Although her eyelids were still puffy from just having woken up, Amber gave her uncle a two-toothed smile. She was an adorable, chunky baby with lengthy pigtails. Boogie had never really been around kids, let alone babies, but there was something about Amber that made him smile. That and the fact that he didn't know Bentley's voice could go to the pitch it was in.

"Shut up, nigga, and c'mon," Bentley said when he noticed the amused look on Boogie's face. He gave his niece one more kiss on the cheek before taking her to her mother. "We'll be out in a minute, Roz."

"Okay. Everything straight?" she asked, slightly raising a brow at him.

"Yeah, shit good. Don't worry about it."

"Whenever you say not to worry about something, it means I need to worry about something."

Bentley waved a hand in her direction, causing her to smack her lips, but she didn't say another word. Boogie was then led through Bentley's nice-sized apartment toward the back. The place was set up nicely with expensive black couches and gold and silver decor along the walls. No one would ever know it was so nice inside just by looking at the building it was in, but Boogie knew that was why Bentley liked it. It was inconspicuous.

When they reached Bentley's bedroom, Bentley hurried to close the door. The natural light beaming in from the outside had the room bright, and the first thing Boogie noticed were the bags of money on the bed. All seeing them did for Boogie was remind him how it was obtained.

"We gotta talk about this," Bentley told him, pointing to the bags of money on the bed. "That nigga Shane is alive."

"Where you see him at?"

"I went to the ER to get stitched up. One of them bullets from last night grazed me, and I didn't know how bad it was until this mornin'. I walked right past his room while he was talkin' to some nigga."

"Did you know the person he was talkin' to?"

"Nah. I was only able to glance in. All I saw was that his face was bandaged up. He had motherfuckas standin' outside his door like he was a prince or some shit. Pretty soon the streets gon' be talkin' about this."

"You sure he gon' be bold enough to be so loud with Caesar lurkin'?"

"You know just like I know that a mouse gon' squeak if the price is right," Bentley told him.

"Well, everybody else who can tell the story is dead."

"Boogie, stop playin' with me. Everybody knows that the only people who could have and would have pulled off some shit like that is Barry's people. It ain't gon' take long for him to come sniffing his nose our direction."

"And if he does, we just finish the job," Boogie said like the answer was so simple. But one look at Bentley's face told him it wasn't. "What's wrong?"

"I did some research on him after I got stitched up. And I found out that we missed somethin'."

"What?"

"Shane isn't who we thought he was," Bentley said. "We figured he was just some low-level hustler tryin'a make a few extra bucks."

"If that ain't who he is, who is he?"

"Shane Hafford. Son of Shamar Hafford."

"Wait." The hair on the back of Boogie's neck stood up. "I know that name. Isn't that—"

"The kingpin of all of Ohio. In other words, Shane is mobbed the fuck up. And if we robbed the kingpin's son, then that means—"

"That we robbed the kingpin," Boogie realized. "Fuck."

Chapter 4

When he got off the plane, Shane Hafford put on the hardest face he could muster despite having a hole in it. The bandage on his cheek covered the stitches, and he was thankful that he didn't have to get his mouth wired shut. The doctors were able to remove the bullet from his jaw in surgery, and all Shane could do was be thankful that his men had to double back because they forgot a bag of money in the car. They arrived too late to catch the thieves but just in time to get Shane to the hospital to save his life. In a sense, he wished they would have just let him die. That blow would have been easier to tell his father, Shamar, than giving him the news that somebody had robbed him and lived to tell the tale.

Once he was cleared to leave the hospital, Shane was on the first flight back to Ohio. For the entire flight, he prepared himself to face his dad and tried to think of what he was going to say. The last thing he needed was for Shamar to find out about his new little addiction. Dabbling in the product was forbidden, and if it was found out that Shane was playing with his nose, the consequences would be dire, especially given the recent play of events. Shamar would cut him off just like he'd done his ex-wife, Shane's mother. However, Shane hoped that they could just bypass all of that when Shamar heard the news Shane had in tow.

When the plane finally touched down, his entourage surrounded him as they moved through the airport. Back home, Shane was a big deal. He was like a prince, and every hustler wanted to be him while every lady wanted to have his baby. He thought he heard a few people call out his name, but he was zoned out as he walked.

Quiet as kept, Shamar had been sending Shane to New York every other month for the past six months. There were some major moves being put into play, and not even Shane had been privy to them all. The only knowledge he was obliged was that his father was in the midst of a huge business deal, one that he needed Shane at the front lines for. While Shane was in New York, it had been his job to find the weakest link in Caesar's camp. It proved difficult because everybody around Caesar was loyal and thorough. His empire was impenetrable. That was when Shane had the idea to go around Caesar's personal empire and focus on the bigger picture.

Shane knew all about the Five Families of New York. Everybody who was somebody knew about them. It was an operation that was envied because many wouldn't have been able to coincide in such peace while making so much money. Greed was something that lived in many men's hearts. Nobody wanted a slice of a pie. They wanted the whole thing. But somehow, the Five Families had managed to turn one whole pie into five whole pies, making New York a gold mine. Even with all the money flowing in and out of the city, somebody had to be unhappy, and Shane had made it his business to find out who.

He spent months doing his research and watching Marco, Li, and Diana move around the state. But it wasn't until Barry Tolliver caught his eye that he made his move. It actually wasn't him that interested Shane. It was his next in command, Julius. He ran into Julius a few months prior, right after scoping out a gentlemen's club run by another head of the Families. The only thing he got from there was the number of the girl with the fattest ass. Other than that, nobody talked too much. He could tell that they had been trained well. They ignored all his questions about Diana. He and his guys had traveled back to Brooklyn to stop at a food spot called Fat John's. It was supposed to have the best loaded barbecue fries, and Shane wanted to see if they had anything on his family's barbecue joint at home. But it seemed fate had placed him in the right place at the right time.

"Yo, Shane, I can't even cap. These fries are good, man. Y'all better ask Fat John for the recipe!"

The voice that spoke belonged to Shane's long-time shooter, Dune. He was pigging out and eating his food like he'd never eaten a day in his life. It was the same with his other shooter, Trent. Shane had to admit that Fat John's gave his family's joint, Barbecue Shack, a run for their money, but he was still rocking with his side. He looked down at his own plate and saw that he'd eaten more than half of his food. He smiled sheepishly.

"Yeah, yeah. Whatever, niggas," he said, wiping his mouth. "What we need to be talkin' about is how we're gon' move this work through here. I can't see an opening nowhere."

"Man. Did you see them choppas that nigga Marco had?" Dune said, referring to the head of the Mexican Family. They'd scoped him out a few days prior at a dock getting a new shipment in. Dune rubbed his hands together and had a dreamy look on his face. "I would love to get my hands on one of them bad boys."

"In due time," Shane told him and dropped his fork. "We still got one more head to pay a visit to. Barry Tolliver."

The information Shamar had given Shane on Barry was that he ran a high-profile theft ring. It was pretty straightforward, but what wasn't mentioned was how off the radar Barry was. He was harder to find than Caesar, and Shane didn't know the first place to look.

While Dune and Trent continued to talk about guns, Shane pulled up a photo of Barry on his burner phone. He didn't have the slightest clue how he was going to find him, and he didn't want to go around asking too many questions and raise alarm. Just as he felt a bubble of annoyance welling up in his chest, the door of the restaurant dinged loudly. Shane glanced up and almost had to wipe his eyes to make sure he was seeing things clearly, but he knew he wasn't dreaming. Walking through the door of Fat John's with a huge smile on his face was Barry Tolliver.

Shane nudged Trent beside him and gave a short nod toward the door.

"Oh, shit," Trent said in a low voice. "That's that nigga right there."

Dune knew better than to turn his head to look, but the expression on his face grew serious. After the initial shock wore off, Shane realized that Barry wasn't alone. Walking beside him to the order counter was a man a head shorter and a few shades lighter. Shane took note of the fact that the look on his face didn't match the happy one on Barry's. Shane watched them from the corner of his eye.

"There goes my favorite customer!" Fat John, the owner and person the restaurant was named after, boomed when he saw Barry.

"Yeah, yeah. You only say that because I gave you the money to start this place up!" Barry said with a laugh.

"You're damn right! But that doesn't mean you aren't my favorite customer. Hell, I wouldn't even have any customers if you hadn't have given me that bag. Well, that bag and the security you keep around the joint."

"Yeah, well. You know I like to look out for my people, and we go way back, my brotha."

"Them grade school days!" Fat John said and then looked at the man with Barry. "Julius, why the long face?"

"I'm just here tryin'a get a bite to eat," Julius answered flatly.

"Yeah, well, let me get right on that, because you lookin' like you might take a bite out of me if I don't!" Fat John grabbed a pad and a pen. "What can I get for you fellas this evening?"

"You already know I want the Fat Attack loaded fries. Extra sauce. Let me get a Sprite to drink. What you getting, Julius?" Barry asked.

"Put me down for two rib sandwiches and a side of macaroni and cheese. You can go ahead and give me a Sprite too."

"A'ight, I'll get these orders out to you shortly," Fat John said after Barry paid.

The two men were handed their drinks, stepped away from the counter, and found a vacant table still in earshot of Shane's table. Shane, Dune, and Trent went back to eating like nothing was out of place, but Shane was listening to every word they were saying.

"Julius, you need to get your head out of your ass. Today was a good day," Barry said, grabbing some napkins for them. "We acquired two new businesses."

"More like blackmailed owners into selling with the computer chip we got from their company on one of Boogie's heists."

"Same difference. Sam and Todd didn't want to have to explain to their wives that they're lovers who like to record their little soirees in the office. They made the right choice by selling. Today should be a happy one."

"And I agree that it is. But it would have been an even better day if you had let me handle the meeting by myself."

"I let you handle a lot of business on your own," Barry said in a dismissive tone. "But this was one that I wanted to be present for. You're still young, Julius. Only ten years older than my son. But when shit happens, you tend to not think. You just react. Imagine how bad things could have gone without me there when Todd was in there talking that shit to you? We would have had a body on our hands just like the last time. And I don't like going into the Family pot to clean up avoidable messes."

"So, what you saying?"

"That when I see you take the streets out of your business decisions, I'll let you do the big deals on your own."

"You mean if Boogie doesn't show up first."

"Now what the hell is that supposed to mean?"

Before Julius could answer, their food was brought to the table. When their server was gone, Julius went to speak, but Barry held his hand up to stop him. He bent his head and said grace, and while he was doing so, Shane watched Julius glare at him. The glare quickly dissolved when Barry lifted his head and dug into his food.

"Now what were you saying, Ju?"

"I was saying, are you sure you're not just keeping me at bay until the person you really want to groom steps up to bat?"

"You know the Pact just like I do. When I step down, everything I've built will go to him. And the same thing will continue when he has children. So yes, I will groom him to take over for me, but that has nothing to do with your position in all of this."

"Don't get me wrong, I love my nephew. But do you really think he's cut out to be a leader? Any chance he gets, he's tryin'a get away from all of this."

"I take full blame for that. I didn't want to raise him to be all about the business like my dad did me. I wanted Boogie to want it, and now that I'm starting to see that spark in his eyes, the grooming can start. Don't count him out before he's in the race. Plus, that boy can find loot in the dark with his hands tied behind his back. Not to mention he can pick any lock created by man. He's been leading his team well, too. So, forgive me if all I see in my son are attributes of a good leader."

"Forgive me if I disagree," Julius told him. "What if . . . what if there comes a time when someone has to take over and Boog isn't ready, then what?"

"Then there would have to be a vote by the heads of the other Families," Barry answered.

"And anybody can be voted as the head of our Family?"

"Not just anybody. They have to be family."

"So, somebody like me?"

"Yes, I guess," Barry said, giving Julius a funny look. "Why are you asking these questions?"

"One thing you should know about me by now is that I like staying ready so I don't have to get ready," Julius said with a serious expression. "I'm as invested in this operation as you are, and I want us to thrive for many years. I don't ever want to see us suffer at the hands of somebody who isn't right for the job."

"Well, it's a good thing we don't have to worry about that for a while. I don't plan on going anywhere for a long time. And, Julius?"

"Yeah, boss?"

"When I took you under my wing all those years ago, I always knew you would grow into a fine businessman. You always finish your jobs and do what you're told. The loyalty you've shown me is all I could ever ask for. But I also need you to know this: some shit you can earn, but other shit you're just born into. You have a good position. Grow in it. But my seat is reserved for my son. And I know one day you'll be as loyal to him as you are to me."

A ringing came from their table, and Barry pulled out a phone from the pocket of his slacks. He looked down at his phone and rubbed his graying head before letting out a sigh. He closed the container of food in front of him and made to get up.

"Is everything good?" Julius asked, seeing the look on Barry's face.

"Yeah. It's Dina. I need to go to the house. You finish eating, enjoy your food, and mull over what I just said."

He patted Julius on his shoulder and squeezed one good time before leaving. Shane hadn't even noticed the two men waiting by the entrance, but apparently they had come with Barry. Upon his exit, one walked in front of him and the other walked behind him, and Shane had no doubt in his mind that they had something on their waists. He had finished his food and was preparing to get up to follow when a voice stopped him.

"I wouldn't do that if I were you."

Shane turned his head and saw Julius staring right at him. "What? I can't leave?"

"Nah. You can't follow Barry," Julius said and flashed the gun on his hip. "Because then I'd have to handle you."

"You ain't the only nigga in here strapped up. And how you figure I'm tryin'a follow . . . Barry, you said his name was?"

"Cut the shit, young'un. I peeped you listening to our every word over there. I know how niggas like you operate. I used to be a nigga like you."

"I doubt it. But I do wanna ask, why would you stick your neck out to defend a motherfucka who just told you that there ain't no room for you to move up the ranks?"

"Yo, who the fuck are you?" Julius asked, not moving his hand from his waist.

Shane saw Trent and Dune make moves toward their own weapons, but Shane held up his hand to stop them. The customers in the restaurant may have been spaced out, but if guns got to singing, there was no telling how many of them would get touched. Plus, Shane didn't see a reason for it to reach that point.

"I ain't introduce myself? How rude of me," Shane said, feigning politeness. "I'm Shane. Shane Hafford."

"Hafford?" Julius asked with a curious look on his face. "I've heard that name."

"I'm sure it's because Shamar Hafford's name rings bells everywhere. I'm his son."

"Hmm. I've heard a lot of things about Shamar. He's thoroughbred."

"At all times. And he always gets what he wants."

"So I've heard. Well, tell me this. Why would the son of Ohio's kingpin be in New York?"

"My father is looking to expand, and the market here is like a feast in his eyes."

"Well, if I know who Shamar is, then you for sure know who Caesar King is. I can let you know right now that ain't gon' happen." Julius chuckled.

"What would you say if I told you he's not gon' be in the picture for very long? Any of them?" Shane asked, and he saw Julius's hand move away from his gun. It was Shane's turn to chuckle. "You must like the little setup y'all have here. To not even have a turf of your own. To just do everything you're told like a little worker ant. Honestly, if I were you, I would hate that shit. You live like a servant, everybody under this Five Families bullshit. The way I see it is if you aren't the head, then you aren't anybody. What are you in charge of? Let me guess. You just oversee all of Barry's dealings, but you have none of your own. How about we change that?"

"There is no way that you can go against the Five Families and win," Julius said, but there was something in his voice that told Shane he was curious to see.

"Are you so sure? We already have our Underground Railroad. We're just lookin' for a guide."

"If you were listening to the conversation between Barry and me closely enough, you heard him speak on how loyal I am. So why shouldn't I go tell Barry what's up right now?"

"Because even loyalty gets tired. I saw the way you looked at him. You want out. Well, I can get you out and his entire empire away from that stupid-ass Pact y'all got. So, what do you say? Are you my guide?"

That was just the beginning. At the time, they were just words for Julius, but after traveling back to Ohio with Shane to meet Shamar, they turned into action. Julius was all in. He was the reason they were able to slip in and out of Brooklyn without being detected. Caesar did business in Brooklyn, but he mostly moved around throughout the other boroughs. Julius told Shane it was because of some disagreement Caesar and Barry had back in the day. For the most part, they stayed out of each other's way, so it was easy for Shane's dope boys to pose as Caesar's and move his product.

Shane was almost to the airport exit when he heard a voice call his name. That time, it was one he recognized. He stopped, forcing his entourage to stop, and looked in the distance to see Julius walking toward him with a Louis Vuitton duffle bag on his shoulder.

"It's about time you touched down," he said and slapped hands with Shane when he reached him.

"Man, you know planes never leave when they say they're gon' leave." Shane shook his head. "My dad probably been out there waitin' for us."

"You told him what happened already?" Julius asked, looking at him.

"Yeah. He ain't say much, so I know that nigga is pissed off. He's the silent but deadly type. Hopefully when I tell him what I gotta tell him, he'll just look at it as a small L. Let's get this shit over with."

They left the airport, and sure enough, there was a shiny black GMC CEO SUV parked right outside the exit. Behind it was another SUV that Shane's entourage was to ride in. Shane couldn't deny that his heart was racing. There was no other man who could put fear into his heart besides his father. He'd shown Shane at an early age that anybody was disposable to him and he could detach himself from anybody and anything. When Shane was younger and would disappoint him, Shamar would break one of his fingers. The pain was to remind him of what side of Shamar's grace he wanted to always be on. It only took five broken fingers. Growing up, Shane feared that Shamar would kill him one day, so every day he lived to please him.

"Welcome home, sir," the Hafford family driver, Dominic, greeted Shane before taking his and Julius's bags.

Dominic opened the door for the men, and Shane allowed Julius to go first. When he climbed in after him, his first sight was of his father calmly sitting in his seat, smoking a Cuban cigar. He looked like an older version of his son, minus the hair, and his style was more choice. Both Shane and Julius sat in the seats facing him. Dominic closed the door behind them, loaded their luggage into the back, and got back into the driver's seat.

Shamar didn't speak until the car was moving. "You have disappointed me, son," he said and took another puff of his cigar.

"I wasn't tryin' to," Shane said. "I ain't think them niggas were gon' be able to get past Dune and Trent. They killed them. They were some of the best shooters to ever stand beside me."

"Cry them a river on your own time," Shamar said in a venomous tone. "My money is missing. So, unless you have it, I suggest you come up with a reason why I still need an heir. Especially one who's gon' have an ugly-ass scar from getting shot in the face."

"Because even though that went bad, we have some good news for you," Shane said, ignoring the sting of his words. "Besides this little setback, everything else is goin' as planned."

"Tell me more," Shamar said. His eyebrow twitched, and Shane knew that as a sign of his interest being piqued.

"It's about Barry," Shane told him.

"He's dead," Julius finished.

After the words were spoken, the only sound heard came from the wind on the highway. Shamar looked from Shane to Julius and then back to Shane. Slowly, a smile formed on his dark lips. That smile soon turned into a laugh.

"That's the best news I've heard all day," he said after his laughter subsided. "I would have rather heard the name Caesar, but that's a start. I'm sure our friends in New York were very happy about that."

"They were," Julius confirmed. "Now that Barry is out of the way, his entire organization will be shaken up, which means the other Families are in disarray too."

"Do you have any idea who could have made the hit on the condo?" Shamar asked Shane.

After he'd gotten hit in the face, he'd fallen to the ground knowing he was a dead man. He kept waiting for the darkness to take him while the commotion around the room continued, but it didn't. Still, in the most excruciating pain he'd ever been in, Shane had lain still on the ground and pretended to be dead. He couldn't see anything that was going on around him because his eyes were closed, but he could hear. And what he'd heard was the masked men drop the ball. On the way out with Shane's money, one of them called the other by his name. That was why, as soon as Shane was cleared from surgery, he went around town getting any information he could on somebody named Boogie. He told his father all of that and pointed at Julius.

"I'd heard the name Boogie before, but it wasn't until Julius came to the hospital that I remembered where I heard it at." Shane put a hand to the bandage on his face and felt an enraged fire in his chest. "Boogie is Barry's son. He's the one who robbed us."

"Is that true?" Shamar asked Julius, who shrugged.

"That's what he says, but I can check and make sure."

"Make sure you do. Barry might have known about our operation the whole time and plotted underneath our noses."

"I doubt it," Julius said. "I would have known about it."

"Either way, I think it's time for me to pay a personal visit to New York."

"For what?" Shane asked.

"War," Shamar said simply.

"We still have to get Caesar out of the way. Even with Barry dead, the other Families are still too strong," Julius pointed out.

"They aren't the only ones with allies, remember." Shamar smirked and averted his eyes to Shane. "Don't you want revenge for what they did to your face? When that bandage comes off, it will be a constant reminder of what was done to you."

Shane touched the tender spot on his face. He knew his dad was right. If Boogie was the one behind the robbery, he would have to die.

It was late evening when Shane finally made it home. He could barely call it that really, especially since he wasn't there much. It was a loft apartment, lavish and spacious. He hadn't even been the one to decorate it, and if it weren't for his belongings, he wouldn't see a pinch of himself there. With ceiling-to-floor sheer gold drapes and the black and gold fancy tapestries on the wall, it wasn't him. Gold wasn't even his favorite color, but it was everywhere, from the wall decor to even his living room tables. But it did make him feel royal whenever he walked through, so he kept it.

He locked the five deadbolts on his door before he kicked his shoes off and removed his gun from his waist, setting it on the dining room table. The wound on his face began to ache badly, and he rubbed it. That only seemed to make it worse. He rummaged in his luggage for the pain medication his doctor had prescribed until he found it. He knew that after he took it, he would be out like a light. He turned to go to the kitchen to get a glass of water, but a movement on the upper level caught his attention. Snatching his gun up in a quickness, he aimed it to the upper level.

"It took you hours to get here, and now you're pointing guns at me?" a woman wearing a sexy lingerie set said with a pout on her kissable lips.

Shane let out a sigh of relief and dropped the pistol back on the table. He was relieved to see Stephanie, a woman he'd met while at the Sugar Trap, standing there. What was supposed to have been a one-time meetup had turned into a full-on fling over the months of him being in and out of New York. She had slanted eyes, plump lips, and a round face with dimples. Her sex appeal was enchanting, and sometimes it felt like she had him under a spell. Not so much that he would ever make her his girl, but if she wanted to throw it back on him, he would catch it every time. With all the moving around with his father and Julius that day, he'd forgotten that he'd put her on a separate flight to meet him in Ohio.

"My bad. It was a long day," he said and grinned as his eyes traveled down her body. The red teddy was shaped like a heart at the top and had black straps that led into a G-string in the back. Her thick thighs looked even more voluptuous at that moment. Shane couldn't lie. His hands were itching to caress her silky honey-nut skin.

She noticed that his eyes were fondling her, and she gave him a seductive smile. "You must like what you see," she teased. "I ordered it from a boutique called Please Me Intimates, and if you hadn't walked through that door when you did, I was for sure about to please myself."

"Well, you ain't gotta do all that now. I'm here."

"Nah, you're there." Stephanie pointed toward the first floor. "I want you here."

She placed her hand between her thighs and gripped her plump pussy. Shane instantly felt his manhood rise. He looked down at the pain medication in his hand and shook his head. His third leg was throbbing harder than the bullet wound under that bandage on his face. Taking the pills would have to wait.

He bounded up the stairs to where Stephanie was waiting hot and ready for him. The first thing he did was take two handfuls of her round bottom and squeeze. He had never bothered to ask if it was natural or bought because he honestly didn't care. It looked good on her and felt even better.

She grabbed his chin and studied his face. "What happened?" she asked, looking at the bandage.

"I got shot a couple of nights ago," he said like it was no big deal.

"Shot! By who?"

"It don't matter. I'm still here."

"Baby, that looks like it hurts," she said in a concerned tone. "Maybe you should rest."

"Hell nah, I got medicine for the pain. Right now, I need some medicine for my dick."

When she opened her mouth to rebut, he stuck his tongue in it. The two shared a sloppy kiss while his hands spread her cheeks wide open. He moved the G-string to the side as his middle finger slid down the crack of her ass until it stopped at the hole. She hissed inside of his mouth when he pushed the tip of his long finger inside of it. He felt her instantly clench up, and it made his rock-hard penis even harder.

"Bend over," he instructed and pointed at the California king behind her.

"What, no foreplay?" She pretended to pout.

"I'm too horny." Shane shook his head. "You knew what you were doing when you put this on."

On the last word of his sentence, he reached and pinched her perky nipples through the red lace of her lingerie. She bit her bottom lip and her eyes slightly rolled at the pleasurable pain. Her reaction turned him on, so he did it again. That time she moaned. Shane grabbed her by the neck, pulling her to him so he could quickly suck on her bottom lip.

"I said turn around," he commanded and threw her on the bed by her neck.

"Yes, daddy," she moaned.

Placing her knees on the edge of the bed, she assumed his favorite position. Shane couldn't lie. Seeing her round ass poking in the air, he knew she was about to get about five good minutes out of him. He could feel the pre cum shooting into his boxer briefs as he watched her arch her back to twerk for him.

"Come onnn, baby! You didn't suck my pussy like I like, so please give me some dick. Right now! Fuck me."

She began spreading her fat pussy lips open for him so that he could see all of the pink wet goodness she had for him. She circled her finger around her engorged clitoris and looked back at him with a sexy grimace on her face. Shane unzipped his pants and pulled out his eight inches of meat. He stroked it a few times before gripping her by her waist and shoving it in. Normally he would have strapped up, especially with a woman like Stephanie, but at that moment he was thinking with his dick. And right then all it wanted was to feel her walls wrapped around it.

What she had begged for was what she got. Shane showed her no mercy as he thrust into her, and it felt so good. Her love cries filled the entire loft, and she kept trying to run from him. Shane wasn't having it. He pulled her back every time.

"You gon' take this dick," he told her and ground into her before hitting her with more deep strokes.

He loved having sex in his loft. Each time he did, it felt like a movie. And at that moment he wished that he had a camera to record the way Stephanie's ass shook each time their bodies connected. He grabbed the back of her pretty blond weave and forced a deeper arch into her back. He took her to pound town, but it wasn't for her. He couldn't care less about her satisfaction. He was chasing his own nut. Suddenly, what felt like an electric jolt going through his body made him jerk. He removed his manhood from inside of her immediately.

"Come on," he said breathlessly, quickly jacking himself.

Stephanie knew the drill. She spun around, placed her lips around his love muscle, and started slurping away. It didn't take long for her to pull his nut out, and Shane threw his head back as he relieved himself at the back of her throat.

"Damnnnn!" he moaned to the ceiling.

She massaged his balls gently and sucked him dry. He heard gulping sounds, and he knew that she was swallowing every drop like a good girl. When the feeling finally passed, Shane stepped away from her and pulled his pants back up. He stumbled to the bed and plopped down, visibly worn out. All he wanted to do at that point was pass out and go to sleep, but now that his erection was gone, the pain in his face screamed loudly again.

"Go get those pills from the table," he said to Stephanie.

He could tell that she wasn't satisfied and probably wanted to reach an orgasm too, but he didn't care. He only had wanted her to come to Ohio to give him a little bit of pleasure while he was there, the same way she had when he was in New York. When she didn't move, he shot her a look that could kill. She rolled her eyes and did as she was told. When she came back, she not only had the bottle of pills but a glass of water, too. He took the items without thanking her. She sat down on the bed and watched him pop two of the pills and down them with the water. When he was done, he placed the bottle and the glass on the nightstand beside the bed. He could feel her eyes on him, but he ignored her. He began to undress so that he could take a shower before the medicine knocked him out for the night.

"Why do you always do that?"

"What you talkin' about?" he asked her in an uninterested tone as he stood up to go to his dresser.

"You know what I'm talkin' about, Shane," she said to his back.

"Nah, I don't. Closed mouths don't get fed. Speak your piece."

"You can be so nice to me, but the moment you get what you want, you switch up and are so mean to me. I thought you liked me, but you don't even care to make me cum."

"Ain't you a ho?" Shane asked bluntly.

"Excuse me?"

"When I met you, you were poppin' pussy in the face of another nigga at a club."

"Well, I'm here, ain't I?"

"Because I like how you pop that pussy." Shane looked at her like she was stupid. "Be grateful you're in my presence. You couldn't really think I would ever want anything more from you."

"But—"

"But what?" Shane turned to face her. "But you expected me to be different from any other nigga who be flyin' you out somewhere? You know what you are. But a'ight, I got you. From here on out, I'ma treat you accordingly. How about that?"

Stephanie sat on the bed, biting back tears. It was clear that she really had grown to care about Shane, but those affections weren't sent back to her. Shane didn't see himself settling down with anybody anytime soon, and when he did, it for sure wasn't going to be with her.

With an armful of clean clothes to change into after his shower, Shane began walking toward the bathroom in the hallway. Right when he got to the door, he stopped and glanced back at her.

"Oh, wait. I actually do need one more thing from you. I need to post up at your spot when I come back to New York."

Chapter 5

Soft, sad crooning filled the Tolliver family house as Boogie stood in the foyer with his mother and grandmother. It was a Tuesday and the day of Barry's funeral. When it was over, all of their family and close friends came to the house for the repast. Barry had only been dead for three days, but Dina told her son that she needed to handle all of the affairs quickly before she lost the nerve. She wanted to say goodbye to her husband before the true realization that he wasn't coming back set in. Boogie still wished she had waited a few days, but he understood. Although he felt numb to everything going on around him, he had to be strong.

"I'm so sorry for your loss," Boogie's older cousin, Alanna, was saying to his mother.

Truth be told, Boogie was tired of hearing the same sentence over and over, but he held his tongue. His dad had a lot of love from all over, and he didn't just take care of the family he made. He took care of everybody, especially if your last name was Tolliver.

"What up, cuz?" Boogie looked away from Alanna to see his cousin Tazz approaching him with his mother, Brook.

Tazz was a self-given nickname for Thomas. He'd always hated his real name, mainly because he was named after a man who'd walked out on him and his mother when he was just a child. Brook had been his father's only sibling and someone he was always overprotective of. Tazz looked like a taller and slightly darker version of Boogie. On his right cheek he had a faint scar from where he had tried and failed at jumping a fence. He was what the girls called sexy chocolate, and he was known for giving them a sweet tooth. Boogie and Tazz were four years apart, with Tazz being older, but they had grown up like brothers. When Boogie and his father had fallen out, the two young men fell off too, not because there was any beef, but because at that moment they were on different paths. However, with the way Tazz embraced him, you would have never known they hadn't talked in months.

"Whatever you need, I got you. Understand? Me and the family," Tazz said as he patted Boogie's back.

"A'ight." Boogie nodded and pulled out of the embrace.

"I'm serious," Tazz told him and glanced at his mother, who was comforting Dina. "Come over here for a second." He nodded his head, motioning for Boogie to step to the side with him. When they were out of earshot of everyone else. Tazz looked seriously into Boogie's face. "I heard whoever was behind this did Unc bad. Said half his face was missin', and his toes were gone. Is that true?"

Boogie had been trying to forget the gory details, but he couldn't. He would forever have the image of his dad lying in the hospital morgue with his chest shredded. He would always know that Barry had died a painful and agonizing death. It ate him up that the only good thing was that he was at least able to have an open casket.

"Cuz, is that true?" Tazz repeated.

"Yeah, it's true," Boogie told him.

"Bet." Tazz clenched his jaw and nodded his head. "I'ma have somethin' for 'em when we find out who did it. Any clue yet?"

"Nah," Boogie told him. "But I'm gon' figure it out. Believe that. And when I do, I'm gon do 'em worse than they did him. Believe that."

"Oh, I believe it. 'Cause I'm gon' be right there. Unc damn near raised me when my own punk-ass daddy was nowhere to be found. I may not feel it as hard as you, but trust me when I say that there is a hole in my chest that won't be filled until blood is shed."

"No doubt. How is Auntie doin'?"

"I would be lyin' if I said she was a'ight. She's goin' through it bad. You know how close she was to her brother," Tazz said, and that time they both looked at Brook. She and Dina were embracing each other and crying softly into each other's shoulders. "She's gon' be all right though. We all will. A'int nothin' we can do but keep his legacy alive. Is Julius here?"

Tazz was referring to Barry's right-hand man and business partner in his theft ring. Boogie looked around for the big light-skinned man but didn't see him. And if he didn't see him, then Boogie was sure he wasn't in the home. There was no way Boogie could have missed the only person too buff for his suit, even in that crowd of people. Julius was another person Barry had taken in and raised. The difference was that he wasn't blood related, but he was still family.

"He was at the church, but I don't think he's here," Boogie noted.

"You know Julius. He doesn't like big crowds. I heard he's in works with the other Family heads to take Barry's spot. You good with that?"

"I didn't know anything about that until you just said it. Maybe it's a temporary thing," Boogie said. "I know he was Pop's right hand and all, but his last name ain't Tolliver. That wouldn't even make sense."

"Well, then that would leave you or me. And we both know how I am with required duties and responsibilities. So that leaves you. It would only be right that his son take over for him. Or are you still tryin'a do your chef thing?"

"I want to, but after this shit with Shane I—" Boogie stopped midsentence, realizing he'd said too much.

"Shane?" Tazz raised a brow at him. "About your age, and just got robbed for doin' business in Brooklyn? Don't even sweat that li'l nigga. I heard Caesar handled him and his crew."

"About that . . ."

Tazz studied Boogie's tired face until he found exactly what he was looking for. When it finally clicked, his eyes got slightly bigger. "Caesar ain't hit that nigga up. You did, didn't you?"

Boogie glanced around to make sure nobody was tuning into their conversation before he nodded his head. Tazz groaned and wiped his hands down his face. "Yo, man. What the fuck were you thinkin'? Do you know who that nigga is?"

"I found out after the hit."

"I didn't think nothin' of it until now because I thought Caesar handled it. What the fuck, Boogie? You know, your pops had a feeling you were doing off-the-record jobs, but now I know you were. Unc would have never sent you on a job like that. Is everything good with that? I heard Shane is still alive."

"It will be," Boogie answered, and they held each other's gaze for a moment before Tazz nodded.

"A'ight. You call me if you need me. I got people."

"I hear you," Boogie said just as he spotted Caesar walk through the front door with a beautiful young woman.

He gave his cousin another embrace before leaving him to go back to his mother. Brook had walked off to speak with their other family members, and Dina had gotten herself together again. He stood beside her and continued to greet people as they came through the door, although his focus was on Caesar. He couldn't remember if he'd been at the funeral.

Boogie's attention then went to the woman he was with. He thought that Caesar was the type to go for a more seasoned woman, but he had to admit that if he were Caesar, he couldn't pass on the one he brought with him either. She was average height for a woman, with a fair skin tone. Her long, natural curls hung loosely to her shoulders, and she had a smile that could brighten up such a sad event. She wore a black dress with a matching hat and veil. Caesar had on a black suit and was holding a bouquet of white roses. Respectfully, they waited their turn in line to offer their well wishes to the family. When it was finally their time to give their love, Caesar handed Dina the bouquet and kissed her cheek.

"Dina, I am so sorry this happened," he said sincerely and took her hands in his. "I want you to know we're doing everything in our power to find out who is responsible."

"I know you are," Dina said, but the smile on her face seemed forced. She turned her attention to the young woman with Caesar. "Milli! I haven't seen you since you were a little girl. Oh, you've grown into such a lovely young lady."

"Thank you, Mrs. Tolliver. And I am so sorry for your loss," Milli said to her in a soft voice.

"I have faith that it will all be sorted out," Dina responded and turned to Boogie. "Boog, this is Caesar's daughter, Amelia. Milli, this is my son, Bryshon. You probably don't remember each other. You only played a few times when you were little."

"It's Boogie," Boogie corrected her. He hated when people called him by his government name, especially if he didn't know them like that.

"Nice to meet you." Milli extended a hand, and he shook it gently.

"You too," he said, looking into her brown eyes and noticing the yellow specks in them. "But I didn't know Caesar had a daughter."

"He keeps me secret," Milli half joked as they let each other's hands go. "I've been away at different schools ever since I could tie my shoes."

"Enough, Amelia," Caesar interrupted, and she smirked. "How about you go with Dina and her mother to the refreshments table so I can speak business with Boogie?"

"Come on, baby. Let us let the men do what they do. Barry's mother makes the best fried chicken in New York. Let's get you some," Dina said, placing a hand on Milli's back and leading her away.

"Is there a place we can talk in private?" Caesar asked when they were gone.

Boogie nodded and motioned for Caesar to follow him to one of the rooms toward the back of the house that had been closed off to guests. It had been Barry's sitting room, but he often referred to it as his man cave. Inside were a large sectional, a big-screen television, and an office desk: the only things he needed, as he also liked to say. The room was where he would come to plan his heists and the heists of all of the people under him. He was a perfectionist all the way down to the time in seconds that it would take to finish a job. It still smelled like his favorite Tom Ford cologne, and inhaling the scent, Boogie realized it was the first time he'd been in that room since before Barry died. He couldn't help but look around and place his hands in his pockets. Everything in the room had seemed so regular to Boogie until then. He never noticed exactly how many photos of him his father had on every wall, from when he was a baby to a man.

"I'm motivated when I'm in my man cave," Barry would say. *"When I'm there, I'm reminded of why I can't fail."* Those words played in Boogie's head, and he quickly turned his back to Caesar. He'd said he wouldn't

shed any more tears for the old man, but it was proving hard.

"It's all right to cry, son," Caesar's voice came from behind him. "Losing a parent is a pain that you can't really put into words. It's more of a hole of sorrow in your chest that doesn't close no matter how you nurse it. Have your moment. I'll just sit down and look at one of these books. Barry always had the strangest book collection. *The Lord of the Rings?*"

Boogie felt himself smile. Barry loved his science fiction. Whenever he had some free time, which was rare, his nose would be buried in a book. Boogie turned back to face Caesar and joined him on the suede sectional.

"He always said that if he fed his mind things different from what his environment had taught him, he would be sharper than the niggas around him," Boogie said. "He always liked being a step ahead of everyone. I guess this time he moved too slow."

"I guess he did," Caesar sighed and placed the novel in his hands on the cushion beside him.

"You figure out who did this yet?"

"Not yet. But I have some people checking into a few things."

"That's not good enough!" Boogie let his emotions get the best of him, and he hit a fist into his palm. "It's almost been a week!"

"Do you think someone would make a hit on one of us and not do well to cover his or her tracks?" Caesar asked calmly. "Trust me when I say I have people everywhere working day and night to figure out who did this. The only thing we can do is be patient. In the meantime, how about you tell me about that hit you made the other night?"

Boogie's anger quickly subsided, and he looked at Caesar with shock in his eyes. He couldn't read Caesar's vibe and didn't know if he should lie or tell the truth. After seconds of pondering what he should do, he shrugged his shoulders.

"I don't know what you're talkin' 'bout," he answered casually, and Caesar scoffed.

"And here I am thinking you had some sense about you. One thing you'll learn about me is that I don't like to ask things twice."

Boogie took in the hard stare coming his way and finally just let out a loud sigh. "A'ight, man. Shit went bad the other night on a job. Two of my boys got dropped, and we barely got away. It was really bad. We . . . we thought we killed the son of Shamar Hafford."

"Well, he's not dead."

"I know."

"He knows your name," Caesar told him calmly.

"What? Impossible."

"I actually don't know if he knows who you are, but if it was this easy for me to figure out who was behind the job, it won't be hard for Shane to. There ain't shit an inquiring mind can't find out for the right price."

Boogie studied Caesar to see if he was joking, but he didn't find one drop of humor there. Plus, if Tazz knew about the hit, then word on the street must have been spreading like wildfire. Still, he couldn't understand how Shane could possibly find out who he was. He'd worn a mask. He racked his mind. There was no way Shane could have known who was there on that hit unless . . .

"That nigga was playin' dead," Boogie said, wiping his hand down his face. "And my man named me to get my attention when my mind was gone. We thought we were the only ones left in that condo. Shit."

"I know for a fact that Barry trained you better than that. Even more, I know Barry wouldn't have sent you on that job. It was sloppy. Who were you working for?"

"Nobody. The nigga who plugged us into the job got killed that night. Me and Bentley just took the money and shook the spot. And then I found out . . . I found out that my dad was dead."

There it was again. Reality. The room grew quiet, and Boogie was once again brought back to real life. He would never look up to see his dad walking into a room again. He would never see Barry's name pop up on his phone again. Boogie inhaled a big breath and forced his thoughts to shift back to the conversation at hand.

"How didn't you know people were moving in on your territory?" Boogie asked Caesar with a slightly furrowed brow.

"That's the thing. I should have."

"Who dropped the ball?"

"Nobody," Caesar told him. "Somebody in my camp is a rat. I'll snuff him out eventually."

"Eventually?"

"Yes, eventually. Right now we have more important things to worry about. Like who killed your father. Oh, and the kingpin of Ohio probably planning to murder you for robbing him and almost murdering his son."

"You say the last part like it's nothing."

"Because to me it isn't. I'm mobbed up. You, on the other hand, aren't."

"What you talkin' about? My pop has a whole army."

"Yeah, one that is only loyal to the head of house. And right now, yours doesn't have one. They won't ride for you. So how about we fix that?"

"Seems like you're already tryin'a fix that. I heard Julius is going for my pop's seat. What's that about?"

"I'm not going to lie to you. Julius has more experience than you in running an operation. He also worked very closely with your father. A few of the other heads think he would be good to take your father's seat. Including me."

"Then why are you here?"

"Because somebody thinks I should give you a chance to prove to me that you are worthy enough to join our table."

"What I gotta do? Have a meeting or somethin' and let 'em know what's up?"

Caesar chuckled. "That was cute, but no. The heads of the other Families, me included, have to vote on the strongest candidate to take over Barry's syndicate. So, as I just said, you have to prove to me that you're worthy. And honestly, kid, right now I'm not impressed."

"Oh, yeah? Well, what I gotta do to impress the almighty Caesar?"

"Ride with me today. Let me put your heart to the test. Back in the day, when your old man was your age, he was a force to be reckoned with. We were a lot alike, actually. That led to us bumping heads a few times, but even with that being said, he was the most sensible of all of us. He had a hot head, but he knew when and how to cool it down. Most men with the power he had think with their ego, but not Barry. We might have had our own separate families, but at that table we were family. He was the part of the scale that balanced the five of us. He made a great leader, and that's going to be something that's hard to follow. So far, in you I'm only seeing the hothead and nothing else. I'm going to give you a chance to prove me wrong."

"A'ight," Boogie said, not backing down. Before, he didn't want to have anything to do with running his dad's business. Now he knew it may be his only saving grace. "Where do we start first?"

"You'll see. Meet me out front in an hour sharp. I'm going to get Amelia home. While I'm doing that, you can take off that suit and put on some street clothes." Caesar stood up and made to go back to the front rooms. "You look like a choirboy."

"But you got a suit on too."

"And I look damn good in it," Caesar replied and was gone.

Chapter 6

The sadness was too loud for Julius as he made his way into Barry and Dina's home from the side door. Everywhere he turned, he saw somebody crying or falling out just like they had at the funeral. He hadn't planned on stopping by the repast, but he knew how suspicious it would look if he didn't show up. It was already bad enough that he had to pretend to be saddened by his death. The mansion smelled like good food, and all he wanted to do was get a plate. Before he did so, he had to go pay his respects to Dina.

"Julius!"

He heard the voice call his name and knew who it was before looking. He stopped walking and turned to see Tazz, Barry's nephew, walking toward him. Tazz was one of the best shooters Julius had ever seen, he had to admit. Julius saw the sadness written all over him and wanted to laugh. Instead, when Tazz finally reached him, the two men shared an embrace.

"Yo, I still can't believe this happened. The shit seems so unreal," Tazz said when they released each other.

"When I got the call, I couldn't believe it. That shit happened too fast. The one time we weren't together," Julius said and sighed sadly.

"What was he even doin' in there?"

"That's where we stashed some of our money," Julius told Tazz with a straight face. "My best guess is somebody found out and there was a robbery."

"Ironic." Tazz shook his head.

"They say we all reap what we sow one day. I just didn't think Barry would reap like this."

"None of us did. But I'm ridin' with Boogie to the top, understand me? The juice is in his hands now, so I gotta stand firm for the Family. Business must continue."

None of you will be standing when I'm through with you, Julius thought. He didn't say anything though. He just nodded his head as if he were agreeing with Tazz. The time would come soon enough for him to reveal what side he was really on.

It had taken years of his life for him to realize that his loyalty to Barry only came from a sense of gratitude. He'd been thankful to Barry for pulling him out of the slums and taking him in. However, he never really sat back to consider if had ever even really liked Barry. Yes, he had been his right hand and even the uncle to his only child, but what did that really mean? That he had played a position with a fake smile on his face for longer than he wanted to. Julius wanted more. He wanted more money, and he wanted more power. He could never reach those heights by being in someone's shadow, someone who had told him that he would be in the same position for the rest of his life. Julius didn't like that Barry had put a cap on him.

"Where is Boogie?" Julius asked.

"I think he went somewhere to talk to Caesar," Tazz answered.

"Fake love always shows its face with death."

"What's that supposed to mean?"

"Nothing you would understand," Julius said and then gave him a stern look. "You know anything about that hit up at the Beau the other night?"

"Nah." Tazz shook his head. "I just heard that the cleanup on it was messy. There was coke all around that motherfucka though, and not the amount you party with. The kind you sell. I'm talkin' bricks on bricks of that good shit. I had to tap in with my people over in Caesar's camp to make sure nobody had taken a go at any of them. But get this: they ain't have no clue about no movements in Brooklyn."

"What happened to all the coke?"

"We gave it to Caesar."

"Why give it to him?" Julius said with a straight face.

"Because that's his area of the game, not mine," Tazz told him in a "duh" fashion. "You got any idea who they were? I mean, they were here in Brooklyn after all."

"Nah. I was gon' ask you the same question. And do you know if any of the people under you had anything to do with the hit?"

"Hell nah." Tazz looked at him like he was crazy. "You know how my unc was. Everything we do is under the radar. He would be pissed right now by how sloppy that job was infiltrated."

"And you didn't recognize none of the bodies that were there?"

"Nah," Tazz said a little too quickly while blinking. "They were all unknown faces."

"You think Boogie had anything to do with it?" Julius finally spat out, growing tired of beating around the bush.

"Boog? Nah, never. I don't think he would do some shit like that. He's too smart."

"Yeah, or just smart enough to cover his tracks," Julius said absentmindedly. "Okay, just let me know if you hear anything."

"Is there a reason you're worried about a hit that got cleaned up?"

"Nah," Julius said with a grin. "Well, besides the fact that for the time being I'm looking over everything. I just want to make sure everything is everything. That's all.

Ain't nothing worse than a snake biting you when you aren't looking."

"I reckon," Tazz said and stared skeptically in Julius's eyes. "Well, I'm about to go check on Auntie."

"You do that. Give her my love," said Julius, grateful for the opportunity to get out of having to pay his respects himself.

"You ain't gon' come over here and speak?"

Julius glanced across the home to where Dina was being consoled by the people around her. He shook his head as he watched the flow of tears leaving her eyes. "No. You know how I feel about crowds. Especially sad ones."

The two men shook hands, and Julius walked out of the home as quickly as he had come in. He'd gotten the answer he was looking for. One thing that made Julius the perfect general was that he paid attention to the details that everyone else overlooked. For example, whenever Tazz told a lie, he talked fast and blinked. It was something Julius had picked up on over the years of working with Barry. As he walked to his cherry red BMW X6 M, he pulled out his phone and dialed a number.

"What did you find out?" Shane said when he answered on the opposite end.

"You were right," Julius said, getting behind the wheel of his vehicle. "It was Boogie."

Chapter 7

Boogie felt bad to leave his mother to entertain the guests by herself, but he didn't feel that he had a choice. What Caesar had said was the truth. Boogie had spent so much time trying to get away from what his dad wanted him to be, he hadn't made any real connections in the world of the underground. He thought things would be like they were in the movies, where the empire automatically went to the oldest son, but apparently not.

Boogie stood in the tall, full-body corner mirror, taking in his appearance. He'd switched into a pair of Amiri jeans and a casual Armani T-shirt. Boogie knew he was a handsome cat, and sometimes that came in handy. Barry had told him to always use his free resources to get what he wanted before digging in his pockets. He'd raised his son to have charm out of this world, even in a pair of jeans and a T-shirt.

Boogie studied his own face, rubbing the thick hair on his chin. He knew Barry would be happy to know that his son wanted to replace him, but the thing was, Boogie knew he didn't want it for the right reasons. He sighed as his mind went to a moment in the first job he'd gone on with his father. He was 18, and he would be lying if he ever said that he wasn't scared out of his mind.

"Did you handle the alarm system?" Barry whispered to his son as he played with the locks on the door.

"I jammed the signal before we got out of the car," Boogie answered.

It was one o'clock in the morning on a Tuesday, and the two of them were dressed in all black. The only holes cut in their masks were for their eyes, and neither could be recognized. In his hands, Barry held two bags filled with things they needed. Boogie glanced around the neighborhood and was glad that the other houses were far enough away to not be able to see them in the shadows. He was even more grateful for the statue in the center of the rounded driveway. It made it easy to hide the unmarked car Boogie and Barry had pulled up in. The home belonged to a man named Douglas Olson. He had come up on Barry's radar because he was a world-renowned diamond collector who happened to live in New York City. He was a single man who lived alone, so Boogie figured it would be an easy hit.

"Pop, you sure he even has any diamonds in his crib?" Boogie asked in a hushed tone. "I mean, they're his prized possession, right?"

"Correction: they're his addiction," Barry schooled him. "So yeah, I'm sure he has diamonds in his home."

Suddenly, the lock he'd been tinkering with clicked, and he turned the knob of the door. He looked quickly back at Boogie, letting him know that it was show time. Wanting to prove himself, Boogie hopped right into action. He knew what he was doing. He just had to rid himself of the fear of getting caught.

He rushed in with his father with his gun drawn in front of him just in case he ran into anyone unexpected. Douglas was out of town that weekend, but still it was wise to take precautionary measures. However, the moment he and Barry reached the stairwell, they came face-to-face with two Dobermans, who had their teeth bared at them.

"Oh, did I mention he has dogs?" Barry told his son with some humor in his tone.

Boogie was too focused on the animals before him to care. The dogs were well groomed and looked as if they'd been trained to protect their daddy's home. He aimed his weapon and prepared to do what he had to do to prevent them from sinking their teeth into his flesh, but he stopped himself when he felt a hand on his arm. He turned to his father, who shook his head. Slowly, Barry reached into one of the bags he was carrying and pulled out a fat steak from a Ziploc bag. He made a few kissing sounds, and when the dogs saw the meat, their demeanor instantly changed. In fact, their tails began to wag, and they licked their lips.

"Y'all want it? Well, here you go!" Barry said to them and tossed the steak in front of the dogs. He turned to his son, and Boogie knew that under the mask he was wearing a smug expression. "I always come prepared."

"That's cool and all, Pops," Boogie said, watching the dogs tear into the meat. "But what about when they're done with it? They're gon' be right back on our asses."

"Can't do that if they're asleep. I put some sedatives in that steak that would knock a tiger out. Now come on. Let's do what we came to do."

Boogie smiled, mainly because he could remember that hit like it was yesterday. They left with diamonds and enough money for Boogie to buy his first luxury car, which he later swapped out for his Ferrari. As he grew older, he knew his father was trying to test his temperature by not telling him there was something unexpected in the house. It was a lesson he took with him: always expect the unexpected. However, on that last job, he didn't know what he had been thinking. He'd let his guard down, the second biggest mistake he could have made as the team's leader. The first was going on the job in the first place. The small smile on his face subsided as reality came back to him. He had a big mess to clean up.

Once he was satisfied with his reflection, Boogie tucked his gun and grabbed his phone. He figured an hour had passed and Caesar would be outside waiting for him. Boogie left his room and was able to creep out of the house without anyone calling his name. Sure enough, parked behind his Ferrari was an all-black Rolls-Royce. Boogie rightfully assumed that it was Caesar's because the driver of the vehicle was holding the door to the back open and looking his way. Boogie made his way to the car and nodded at the driver before getting into the back passenger's side.

"I've been out here waiting for ten minutes," Caesar said once Boogie's door was shut. "I thought I said one hour." He sat next to Boogie in the same suit, wearing a hard expression on his face.

"My bad. I lost track of time. I was thinkin' about my dad," Boogie answered honestly. "About the first job we ever went on together."

"Well, this is the first job we've ever been on. And when I do business, I like to be prompt," Caesar told him, although the expression he wore softened slightly. He turned his focus to his driver through the divider. "Bring us to Minny's spot, Clarence."

"Yes, sir," Clarence said and pulled away from the house.

Caesar rolled up the divider window and turned his head to look out the window. Boogie didn't know what he expected, maybe a little conversation or an explanation of what exactly Caesar expected him to do. After a few minutes went past, Boogie finally cleared his throat. "So, who's Minny?"

"A man I'm about to murder," Caesar told him flatly.

"Oh," Boogie said and tried not to sound shocked, mainly because somehow, he knew Caesar was serious. "Why?"

"The same reason most people lose their lives in this game: bad business. It's better to kill a sick dog than to give him medicine, because you'll just be nursing him back to health for him to bite you again."

"I feel that."

"You feel that, huh? Tell me something, Boogie. What do you want?" Caesar asked with his eyes still out the window.

"Is that supposed to be a trick question?" Boogie responded. "I want a lot of things."

"I'll be more specific then. Are you really built for this kind of life? Or do you still want to be a cook?"

"How can you ask me if I'm built for the life I was born into?" Boogie didn't mean for the question to come out sounding so harsh, but it did. "The real question is, am I built to be a chef? And the answer to that would be no, it's just something I like to do. It's something I chose to do."

"So, if it came down to choice, you would choose to leave all this behind and be a chef, instead of in this car with me?" Caesar asked and finally turned to face him. He looked curious.

"It's not that simple anymore."

"But isn't it?"

"Nah," Boogie sighed. "My pops' empire may not have been somethin' I chose. But if it's between givin' it to me or someone else, I'm willin' to give up that dream. For now, anyways. I can always come back to that. But this? If I give it up, it will be gone forever, and that ain't worth it. If anybody is gon' be sittin' at that table in his place, it's gon' be me."

"Are you saying that because you really want to be voted as a leader of Barry's syndicate or because you happen to find yourself currently in a bit of a bind?"

"I'm not ashamed to say a little bit of both," Boogie told him. "But either way, I'm ready to prove my worth."

To that Caesar said nothing, and that time it was Boogie who turned his attention to the views outside the car. He had lost track of time, but it seemed like forever had passed when they finally pulled up to their destination. Clarence parked in the parking lot of a food spot that was attached to a liquor store. Both buildings had the name MINNY's on them and had the same chipping on their painted white brick. Boogie got out of the car after Caesar and followed his lead to the door of the barbecue joint. Standing outside was a big man with a bald head and eye patch. It wasn't something Boogie expected to see, and he had to stifle his laugh.

"Somethin' funny, youngsta?" the man growled, noticing Boogie's smirk, and then he spat at his feet.

"Somethin' like you?" Boogie asked, making a face at the chewing tobacco by his Jordans. "C'mon. You standin' out here in a dirty white shirt and an eye patch. Who you s'posed to intimidate, Popeye?"

"You should ask your mama. She was the one runnin' from all this dick last night," the man said, spitting again.

Boogie took a step forward, but Caesar placed a hand on his chest to stop him. It was the bald man's turn to laugh. He didn't seem to be at all fazed by the deathly stare Boogie was giving him.

"Leave the boy's mama out of it, Dennis," Caesar warned. "It ain't nobody's fault but yours that you're standing out here looking like a cyclops after you got yourself shot in the eye last year. Now get the fuck outta my way so I can speak with Minny."

"Yes, sir," Dennis said quickly and stepped out of the way.

Once they were inside, Boogie shot another mean look over his shoulder before following Caesar through the dark restaurant. Instead of tables, Minny's had benches and was lit up by red lights. Smooth R&B was playing softly from the restaurant's speakers, and there were a few patrons to each table. Many whispered among themselves as Caesar and Boogie passed:

"Who is that kid with Caesar?"

"That's Barry's boy, I think. You heard somebody killed him, right? Heard they had to have a closed casket."

Boogie ignored them, but his jaw clenched tightly. He had to remind himself that he was there for business and not to fight everybody who had something to say about his parents.

He and Caesar made their way to the back of the restaurant, past the kitchen, and to a dimly lit hallway. At the end was a door that had two more big goons standing outside of it. Upon seeing Caesar, they stood up straighter. Boogie saw that they also were slightly positioned more in front of the door than they were before.

"Minny stepped out for a minute," one of them said in a guff voice.

"He stepped out for a minute?" Caesar repeated.

"Yeah," the other said. "So why don't you stop back a little later? He said he'd be back later today."

"Y'all must think I'm stupid. If he ain't here, what the fuck are y'all guarding behind that door?"

Caesar took one step toward them, and they both looked at each other as if trying to figure out what to do. Boogie had never seen Caesar in action, but he'd heard the stories. And apparently both men knew who they were dealing with. When he got too close, the men scattered up the hallway like roaches.

"Y'all know y'all probably fired, right?" Boogie called after them as Caesar opened the office door.

The aroma of warm cigar smoke hit Boogie's nostrils, but when he looked over Caesar's shoulders there was nobody in sight, just a lit overhead light, a messy desk, and a cozy chair in the corner. If somebody had made a clean getaway, Boogie couldn't see where they would go. There wasn't even a window. And unless Minny was a midget, he couldn't see him climbing through the vents either. Caesar calmly walked over to the desk and sat on it with his back toward Boogie. He tapped on it with his fingers a few times before looking down in front of the empty desk chair.

"Minny, get your big ass up from under that desk," Caesar said to someone Boogie couldn't see.

Boogie heard grunting, and a few moments later, a husky man with a crisp hairline materialized behind the desk. Where he stood, he was face-to-face with Caesar, and you would have thought he had seen a ghost the way his light face was flushed. He looked toward the door as if he wanted to make a run for it, but he saw Boogie standing in front of it.

"There's nowhere to run, Minny," Caesar sighed and dusted off the shoulder of Minny's gray suit. "Now I've given you enough time. Where is my money?"

"Caesar, c'mon, man. I just need a little more time," Minny stammered, and Boogie saw the gleam of the one gold tooth in his mouth. "You know I'm good for it."

"No, you were good for it. That was before you started hanging with the Italians and gambling all your money away. Excuse me, my money. Now what, you need some more time because you have to pay your debt to me and get yourself out of that hole you got yourself in with the Italians?"

Minny's silence let Boogie know that what Caesar said was true. The air conditioning had already been on in the office, but suddenly it felt frigid.

"Where's my money, Minny?" Caesar asked again.

"I don't have nothin' right now, Caesar. If you just give me another few days—"

"So, you're broke? You mean to tell me you have two profiting businesses and you're broke?"

"It seems that way. But please, Ceez, I'll pay you the fifty grand I owe you in a few days."

Caesar eyed Minny down for a few moments before smiling. He then extended his arm for Boogie to come to the desk, which he did. Minny's eyes instantly went to Boogie's hands, perhaps to check for a weapon, which he didn't have. Not in his hands anyway.

"Minny, we go way back, don't we?"

"Yeah, we used to kick it way back when."

"So, you remember Barry, right?"

"How could I forget? The two of you used to be friends back in the day," Minny answered.

Boogie's brow lifted when he heard that. He knew Caesar and his father knew each other on the business tip, but not as friends. That was something his father never talked about, nor did Caesar think to mention it.

"Okay," Caesar continued. "So, if you remember that, do you remember that game Barry and I used to play when we were in a room with a bunch of motherfuckas?"

"Yeah. The two of you would guess who was the richest in the room. Each of you would pick one person as your champion. You would always go for the best-groomed person, but Barry had a different way of studying people. He knew material things didn't always equate to that big bag. He always won that game."

"And do you remember how we would find out who won?"

"Yes. Barry would rob them."

"Now, Minny, if your ability to pay debts were as good as your memory, I wouldn't be here right now," Caesar said with a little chuckle. "I want to introduce you to somebody. This is Boogie. Boogie Tolliver."

"B . . . Barry's son?" Minny asked.

"Yeah. He only had one of those. One he passed all his knowledge down to. Did your old man ever teach you that game?" Caesar asked Boogie.

"It wasn't really a game," said Boogie. "He just taught me how to spot how much money a person had just by watchin' 'em. It was how I was supposed to calculate my licks."

"Well, humor me. How much money you think this greasy motherfucka has?"

Boogie looked at Minny and then back at Caesar, who gave him an encouraging nod. Slowly, he walked around the desk to get a better look at Minny. Boogie looked from the shiny curls on his head, to the shiny gold watch on his wrist, all the way down to the Stacy Adams on his feet. After observing him for a few moments, Boogie went back to where he'd been standing.

"Well?" Caesar asked.

"He ain't got much," Boogie answered, "given the last-season suit and the fake Rolex on his arm. But that doesn't mean that he ain't got nothin'. Even with a gamblin' problem. The fact that it's a random Tuesday and he pretty much has a packed house lets me know the food here must be good. Which means he has a pretty good monthly income. I'm assumin' this and the liquor store next to it are owned, so all profit goes straight into his pockets. So rich? Nah. Broke? Never. Even a bad gambler stashes some ducats away."

"And if you were that bad gambler, where would you stash your little paper?"

"My pops used to always joke and tell me never to stash cash where I lay. And I would ask him, why not? And he would tell me that was how most niggas think. You can always find a safe or a little money stash next to a nigga's bed or his favorite seat."

On his last sentence, Boogie walked casually over to the couch in the corner of the room. Behind it, there was a square vent close to the floor that was big enough to hide something in. And when Boogie knelt and tugged on the metal brackets, they came apart from the wall without much force. Inside, seemingly waiting for him, was a safe. He picked it up and brought it to the desk.

Minny's eyes were wide as he watched Boogie play with the dial. It wasn't hard to crack that safe. It was one of those standard ones anyone could get from a grocery store.

"Caesar, I—" Minny tried to say when Boogie swung the door open.

Caesar held up his hand to silence him as he stood up from the desk and turned his back to him. Boogie turned the safe to face him, and Caesar let out a breath as he stared at the stacks of hundreds inside along with a small pistol.

"That . . . I didn't know there was that much money there. I put a couple thousand up here and there for emergencies," Minny lied through his teeth, and Caesar let out another long breath.

"Unlike you, Minny, I am a man of my word. You owe me fifty thousand, so that is what I am going to take from your stash. Plus a finder's fee, of course. Boogie, hurry and count out sixty thousand dollars so that we can go."

Boogie didn't understand. There had to be at least $100,000 in the safe. "Sixty thousand? Why leave any behind?" he asked but did as he was told.

"So that his family can have some money for the funeral."

Pfft!

Boogie's eyes had been on the money, so he didn't see that Caesar had reached into his pocket. Nor did he see him screw the silencer on to his pistol. What Boogie did see was Minny folding to the ground like a towel with his eyes rolled back. Casually, Caesar blew on the smoking gun before tucking it back into his pants. Boogie dumped out the little bit of trash Minny had in the wastebasket by the desk and put the stacks of money in it.

"Welp, this should be sixty bands," Boogie said, taking the bag out and holding it up. "How about we get out of here?"

Boogie walked quickly to the hallway while Caesar took his time leaving the room. Although Caesar had told him that he was going to murder Minny, Boogie paid attention to how second nature it had been to him.

"Yo, you hot out here," Boogie chastised Caesar when he finally got to the hallway. He was angry, and in his anger, he'd forgotten who he was talking to. "You can't just be killing people like that! There were customers in there. What if somebody had come back here?"

"They would have pretended they didn't see anything. Because just like I killed Minny, I could touch their entire families." Caesar smoothly stepped past Boogie.

They left the same way they'd come in, and Clarence was standing outside the Rolls-Royce waiting for them. When they were inside the car, Boogie gave the bag of money to Caesar and leaned back in his seat. Shortly after, he felt something hit his lap. When he looked down, he saw that it was a stack of money.

"Your finder's fee," Caesar told him.

"I figured you'd hold on to it until we were done making your rounds," Boogie said with his eyes closed.

"Never been one to hold on to what isn't mine."

"Well, in that case, I'll just put it under the seat and hope that Clarence doesn't rob me."

"Clarence gets paid handsomely. He wouldn't even bat his eye at a dollar," Caesar told him.

"Yeah, maybe," Boogie said, opening his eyes and looking at Caesar. "Why didn't you tell me that you and my pops was tight back in the day?"

"It never came up."

"I guess it never came up for him either, because he never said too much about you. Did y'all fall out or somethin'?"

"Or something," Caesar said. "You did good back there, Boogie. Barry would have been proud. Minny was shaking in his boots when you pulled that safe from the vent. Your old man trained you well."

"Thank you. Now what?"

"Now I need you to do what you just did at three more stops."

Chapter 8

It was almost one in the morning when Boogie finally got home. Not only had he helped Caesar collect all the money that was owed him, but he made a nice piece of change in the process. He was also glad that there had only been one casualty in the process.

Upon entering his home, the first place he went was the guest bedroom. He flicked on the light and was met with a sight of teal and silver. No one ever stayed at his house, but the room was still fully furnished with a bed, a desk, and wall decor. The headboard of the queen-sized bed was against the wall, and the mattress set sat up high. Boogie sighed as he plopped down on the bed and looked at the cash in his hands. He felt his mind drifting to thoughts he didn't want to have at the moment, so he quickly did what he came to do. Pulling the thick comforter up and peeling the sheets back, Boogie felt for an incision in the mattress. It was small but big enough to stuff the money through. Once he was done, he put the covers back the way they were, got up to turn the light off, and left the room.

He didn't know exactly how much money was in the mattress, but it had to be close to $1 million. He'd been stashing money away for almost two years. Boogie hated keeping that much money where he laid his head, but he couldn't exactly get a bank account with that kind of money. With Barry dead, it meant that his stream of small businesses went to his wife and Boogie. However, those were some of the things he didn't want to think about. He didn't know anything about running businesses or taking his father's place in the underground world. He would just have to take it day by day.

After showering in the master bathroom connected to his room and throwing on a pair of Versace briefs, Boogie fell back onto his California king bed. His body melted into the Tempur-Pedic mattress as it adjusted to his form, and he felt his body instantly relax. As his eyes closed, he clapped his hands twice, and the bright light coming from the fixture on the ceiling turned off. Sleep was almost his friend until he heard the violent vibration of his phone coming from the nightstand beside his bed. Groaning, he rolled over to grab the cell and fought the urge to launch it across the room so he could get some rest.

"Hello?" he answered without looking at the screen.

Silence.

"Hello?" he repeated, but once again he was met with the same nothing. "A'ight. I don't like people playin' on my—"

"Hello?" a woman's voice came rushing through. "Hello? My bad, my phone was on mute. Can you hear me?"

"Yeah, I can hear you. Who is this?" Boogie asked, rubbing his eyes.

"Roz."

When he heard her say her name, Boogie sat up on his elbow. She was the last person he expected to hear from, let alone call him directly, even though it was true her face had crossed his mind a time or two after coming across her. "Roz?" Boogie pretended not to know who she was.

"Boy, don't play with me. I can hang up this phone right now." She smacked her lips.

"A'ight, a'ight. I quit," Boogie said with a small laugh. "What's poppin', shorty? How'd you get this number?"

"I got it from my brother's phone the other day."

"Hmm, the other day, huh? Well, why has it taken this long for you to hit me up?"

"You know why."

"I don't. So, tell me somethin'."

"Because I can tell that you know you cute. And you probably have bitches sniffing at your little ashy heels. So, I didn't want to look thirsty," she admitted.

"Well, I like your honesty. But, nah. I don't really give females this number like that. Next thing you know, they're callin' you at almost two in the mornin'," he joked.

"Ha-ha, real funny. I'm only calling now because I just got my baby to bed."

"Aw damn, she runs that household, huh?"

"Man, listen! Shit doesn't move until Miss Amber says so!" Roz said, and Boogie could hear the smile in her voice. "But you're right, it's late, so I guess I can make this quick. I don't know what kind of shit you and my brother got going on, but he just tossed me thirty bands today like it was nothing, so I know it's something major. All I ask is that you look out for him. We're all we got."

"You ain't got to worry about that. I got him, especially if he got me," Boogie reassured her without going into too much detail.

"Good."

Things got quiet for a moment before Boogie spoke again. "That's all you wanted?"

"Yeah," she said at first but then switched her answer. "No. Actually, I was wondering if you wanted to—"

"Tomorrow night, be ready by eight," Boogie cut her off. "Wear somethin' nice. Text me the address."

"How'd you know what I wanted to ask?"

"I'm handsome, and girls be sniffin' around my ashy-ass ankles, remember?" Boogie smiled and disconnected the call.

He didn't know Roz well at all, but what he could tell from his brief encounter was that she probably wouldn't take well to being hung up on. However, moments later his phone vibrated, and a text message formed on the screen. He read it and laughed out loud. It was her address, but attached to the message was a GIF of a woman smacking a man out of his seat. Boogie dropped the phone on the bed beside him so that he could finally go to sleep.

Step back. You're dancing kinda close.
I feel a little poke coming through on you.

The catchy Next song sneaked its way into Boogie's ears as he lay fast asleep in his bed. It took a few moments for him to realize that the music wasn't a part of his dream, and once he did, his eyes snapped open. He was lying flat on his back, staring at the ceiling, his ceiling. He was in his room, and to make sure of that, he glanced around at the familiar surroundings. Boogie knew he hadn't left any of his speakers on the night before, but still the music was coming from somewhere. Not just the music. Boogie sniffed the air as he sat up and recognized the smell of bacon being fried in his kitchen.

"What the fu . . ." Boogie's voice trailed off as he reached under his pillow and grabbed his piece.

He threw his covers to the side and got out of bed wearing only a pair of pajama pants. He didn't know who was in his home, but they were going to learn that they'd broken into the wrong spot. Boogie crept down the hallway, and the music got louder and louder the closer he got to the source. Cocking his gun right before he emerged from the end of the hall, he prepared to shoot the tall man hovering over the stove in the kitchen.

"I'd think twice about that if I were you," the man spoke loudly with his back still to Boogie.

Instantly, Boogie let out a breath and let his arm drop to his side. He should have recognized the expensive suit, but he was still a little groggy. If Caesar hadn't spoken, he would have had a bullet in the back of his head.

"Ay, man, what the hell are you doin' in here?"

"Making breakfast," Caesar answered as if Boogie had just asked a stupid question.

"I see that, but why?"

"Because it's the most important meal of the day. Sit down. Everything just got done."

Boogie looked from Caesar maneuvering around in the kitchen like he owned the place to the dining room table. He contemplated telling Caesar to get out of his apartment, but he figured that wouldn't be the smartest thing to do, especially since he didn't know how Caesar had even found out where he lived. Reluctantly, he sat down at the table and waited for Caesar to put in front of him a plate containing an omelet, bacon, and toast. He had to admit, it looked as delicious as it smelled. Caesar sat across from him at the glass table with his own plate and a jug of orange juice from Boogie's refrigerator.

"How did you find out where I stay? And how did you get in?" Boogie asked, but Caesar held up a finger.

He closed his eyes and bowed his head for some time. Boogie assumed that he was saying his grace, something that his father always did before every meal. In fact, he did it just that way Caesar did. Barry never clasped his hands together. He would simply bow his head. He would say that putting his hands together made him feel as if he were begging when all he wanted to do was give thanks. With all the ugly he'd put into the world, he was still blessed to have everything he needed, and for that he was grateful.

When Caesar finally lifted his head, he stared across the table at Boogie. "I find out anything I want to know," he answered and then smiled. "And you weren't the only one your old man taught how to pick a lock."

"That's coo' and all, but you ain't got breakfast at your own crib?" Boogie asked, taking a big bite out of his omelet.

"Of course I do. I'm rich. But I figured I'd come over here since we have a stop to make today. You aren't done proving yourself to me."

"Today?" Boogie stopped chewing. "Like all day?"

"Maybe. Money never sleeps."

"I can't today. I have plans."

"Well, if you want the seat at the table, keep in mind that time is of the essence. We have decided to vote in one month."

"A month? We buried my pops yesterday. Whose gon' run his business?"

"I'm sure your father had very capable people around him. Julius has been running the show, and it hasn't fallen to collapse yet, so it probably won't. Which means we have time."

"Time for what?"

"Time to see if you're built to fill the void your father has left in the game. But of course, if something is more important, be my guest. Go handle that."

Boogie thought of Roz and about their date that night. He knew if that day went the way the prior had gone, he wouldn't be getting in until well past eight o'clock. That meant that before anything could even begin between him and Roz, he was going to let her down. Hopefully she would get over it.

"A'ight, whatever. What we gotta do today?"

"I thought you'd make the right decision," Caesar said with an approving undertone. "Our first stop is at a place that you know well."

"Oh, yeah? And where is that?"

"The cleaners your family owns."

"Fast Cleaners?"

"That's the one."

"Why are we going there? If somethin' was wrong, Mama would let me know."

"Unless she was the something wrong."

Caesar's comment made Boogie put his fork down on his half-eaten plate. "What you talkin' about?"

"A business colleague of mine called me up this morning looking to sell me a property in Brooklyn that he is about to acquire from a buddy of his named Arnold. Imagine my surprise when I found out the property in question was none other than Fast Cleaners. Arnold said he would be meeting with the owner's widow and signing the deed this morning. With the price your mother put on the place, she's trying to get rid of it quick."

"But she wouldn't do that." Boogie shook his head, trying to make sense of it all. "We just buried my dad. Why would she—"

"Our best bet is getting down there right now before the ink is dry."

"Let me throw on some clothes real quick," Boogie agreed and pushed away from the table. "I'll be ten minutes."

While he was in his bedroom getting dressed, Boogie tried to run down all the reasons his mother would be trying to sell the cleaners. Not only had it been in the family for years, but it was the first business Barry had ever owned. Even though it wasn't bringing in as much business as the auto shop, the hair salon, or the many other businesses the family owned, he would have thought Fast Cleaners held some sentimental value. He wasn't happy about Dina making that kind of decision without him. Barry hadn't even been in the ground a full twenty-four hours.

"I'm ready," he said when he came out of the room wearing a comfortable gray sweat suit and a pair of crisp all-white Air Force Ones.

Caesar took one look at him and sighed disappointedly. Boogie, taken aback, stared down at his outfit, trying to figure out the problem. "What?" he asked.

"You look like a thug."

"A thug? This is Armani. Bitches love shit like this," Boogie told him, outwardly offended.

"Labels don't mean anything to sharks in the water getting the same kind of money you are. The tone is set by the aesthetic you present. And right now, you're giving me dope-boy vibes."

"That sounds ironic coming from the kingpin himself."

"Except I don't look like a kingpin. I look like a CEO. You'll learn. Right now, we have other things to attend to besides your poor sense of style."

Boogie bit the inside of his cheek to stop himself from saying something uncalled for and outlandish. Caesar was right. They had bigger things to attend to.

They left Boogie's condo in Caesar's car and headed in the direction of the cleaners. That day, Caesar was driving a chromed-out BMW coupe. Boogie leaned back in the seat and enjoyed the ride on the interstate. The car went fast, but not nearly as fast as his. Still, Caesar weaved through traffic like a pro and got them to their destination in record time.

"You musta wanted to be a NASCAR driver growin' up or something, huh?" Boogie asked after they parked and got out of the car.

"No. But I did used to race at night back in the day," Caesar told him with a chuckle.

"*Fast & Furious* ain't have shit on you, I bet," Boogie joked, and Caesar laughed some more.

"Damn right! Now come on, boy. Let's see if Dina is up in here."

"She is," Boogie noted, nodding at the yellow Jeep Wrangler parked directly in front of the nicely kept building.

Before they got to the door, Boogie glanced inside the cleaners and saw the employees behind the desk busy at work. In a far corner, sitting at the small waiting table, was his mother, a white man next to her, and some uppity-looking black man across from them. Judging by the look of the paperwork in front of them and the serious expressions on their faces, they must have been in the middle of discussing something important.

With Caesar not too far behind him, Boogie pulled the door open, causing it to chime. All eyes turned to them, and the young lady behind the desk batted her eyelashes at him. Her name was Gia, and Barry had hired her two years prior when she was 18. Not much had changed about her except that she'd gotten her braces taken off. She'd had a schoolgirl crush on Boogie back then, and judging by the dreamy look on her face, she still did.

"Hey, Boogie," she gushed when he walked in. "Long time no see. You must be doing good for yourself. You rolling with Caesar and all."

"I'm just tryin'a make some things shake, that's all."

"Uh-huh. Well, we all know how Caesar gets down. You just be careful, a'ight? And I'm sorry to hear about Barry. He was a good man."

"Thank you, Gia," Boogie told her.

"No, thank you for keeping all of us on as employees. We ain't know what was gonna happen when he passed. We thought you might try to sell this place."

"That's actually what I'm here to see about right now," Boogie said and averted his attention to his mother.

Dina had seen her son when he first came in. She had the face of a child when they were caught red-handed doing something they weren't supposed to be doing. She blinked a few times, and it was obvious that this was the last place she expected to see her son. Boogie forced a smile on his face while Caesar took a seat in one of the other waiting chairs. When he approached the table his mother was at, the men sitting with her looked up to see who had just walked up on them.

"If you don't mind, we're trying to conduct business here," the white man sitting beside Dina said in a dismissive tone.

"Well, when it comes to conducting business about my father's cleaners, I think it's important that I be here. Don't you think so, Mama?" Boogie cut his eyes at Dina and extended a hand. "My name is Bryshon Tolliver, and you are?"

"My name is Henry Booker." The man paused to clear his throat and glance down at his paperwork. "It's nice to meet you, Bryshon. I handle all of your father's estates. And yes, I see your name listed here as part owner of all of your father's businesses. I'm sure it was a hard decision to part with Fast Cleaners but—"

"You must have me confused with another Bryshon Tolliver, because I haven't made a decision about a goddamn thing," Boogie said, cutting his eyes at him.

"Boogie, wh . . . what are you doing here?" Dina butted in and tried to grab his arm, but he pulled away.

"What do you mean, what am I doing here? The question is really, what are you doing here? And what the fuck is Harry talkin' about?"

"It's Henry," Henry corrected him and pointed at a line on his paperwork. "And it shows here that you signed over ownership of the cleaners so that your mother could sell it."

"Mama, my signature better not be on this fuckin' paper," Boogie warned his mom as he snatched the paper up. Deep down he was hoping that Henry wasn't telling the truth, but when Boogie saw a scribble of what was supposed to be his signature, he knew there was no lie. "Yo, what the fuck are you doin', Mama?" He threw the paper back down on the table and glared at her. How could she forge his signature?

"Boy, don't you ever talk to me like that!" she exclaimed and jumped to her feet. "This is my business, and I can sell it if I want to!"

"Not with my forged signature you can't," he growled.

"Forged?" Henry stated in an alarmed tone.

"You know what? This is getting awkward. I'm gonna go." The black man at the table stood up, but Dina grabbed his arm.

"No, Arnold, stay. We can close today," she almost begged.

"With all due respect, Dina, I don't want my name on any paperwork with a forged signature. Things can get messy that way."

"I think I'm going to leave as well and let the two of you work things out," Henry said and gathered all of his paperwork. "Dina, you have my number. Bryshon, it was nice meeting you. My condolences about your father."

The two men walked out together, but Boogie was too busy giving his mother a mean stare down to care. He took notice of the disappointed look on her face. Words seemed to fail her, but that was okay because he had a lot to say.

"What were you thinkin'? You had to know I was gon' find out about this."

"I figured that it would be after the ink dried," she said honestly and snatched her red Balenciaga bag off the table.

"And you were never gon' tell me that I'm part owner of all of Pop's businesses, too, huh?"

"If your father didn't tell you, why would I?" she said tersely, getting up and placing her hand on her hip over the suit jacket.

"The dirt over his coffin is still soft, and you're already makin' moves to do away with his legacy."

"Listen here, boy. I love you to death, but you have one last time to use that tone with me. Your father is dead, and no time limit of grieving is going to change that. Barry is gone, Boog. He's gone. That means I can do whatever with all of this. I don't have a job or a degree. I don't know the first thing about running none of these businesses! So no, I don't want them. I just want to do away with them. All of them!"

"So that's what this is about?" Boogie asked, and he felt his demeanor soften. "You're worried about money, Mama? I thought you and Pops had money in the bank."

"It's not about that! It's about the fact that I don't want to be responsible for any of this anymore. I just have to do something. Something I can control." Dina choked up on the last word and wrung her hands in front of her. "I don't want to hold on to anything that reminds me of Barry. I can't. I can barely stand to be in that house!"

She took a few deep breaths to steady herself because the one thing Dina Tolliver didn't do was cry in public. Seeing her so off-balance washed away the anger Boogie had toward her moments before. He took her hands in his and gave her a reassuring look.

"Mama, you ain't gotta worry about none of that. You know I'm gon' make sure that everything is taken care of the way Pop would have wanted me to. Especially now that I know I'm an owner. I got it. I got us, forever."

"Unless you go and get yourself killed too! Especially if you plan on following in your father's footsteps." Dina shot a distasteful look over Boogie's shoulder at Caesar. "You still don't know who did this. What if they're after you too?"

"I'ma be careful, Mama. Don't worry about me. Matter of fact, don't worry about nothing. Why don't you go stay with your sister for a while? Detox a bit from the house, okay? Because we aren't selling the cleaners, or anything for that matter. Especially not for pennies if you're worried about money. Trust me, a'ight?"

"Okay," Dina sighed and shrugged her shoulders. "Okay."

The two of them embraced before she went for the exit. Caesar nodded at her in respect, but she just pursed her lips and walked right by him. It was an odd exchange, especially since the two seemed cordial at the funeral. But Boogie brushed it off as his mother just being a firecracker when things didn't go her way.

As he watched her walk toward the door, Boogie also noticed a black Cadillac Escalade slow up in front of the cleaners. The hair on the back of his neck stood up because something just didn't seem right about it. Caesar saw the look on his face and turned his gaze to what Boogie was looking at. The front and back passenger windows of the Escalade rolled down, and Boogie took a brisk breath when he saw Shane staring dead at him from the back seat. He and his shooter in the front seat had two AK-47 assault rifles pointed at the front of the business.

"Mama! Get down!" Boogie shouted right before the gunshots rang out.

He leaped and grabbed her just in time to pull her to the ground as the bullets ripped through the place. The workers behind the desk screamed bloody murder, but there was nothing that Boogie could do about it. It seemed to go on forever, and Boogie shielded his mother's body with his own. Finally the gunfire ceased, and he heard the sound of tires squealing on pavement as the Escalade drove away. Boogie slowly lifted his head and saw Caesar standing and dusting the debris from his suit.

"Get up, boy. They're gone," he confirmed to Boogie.

"Come on, Mama," Boogie said, pulling his shaky mother to her feet.

She clung tightly to him, almost as if she were afraid to let him go. She looked around wide-eyed at all of the damage that had been done just that fast. Her lips trembled, and she held her son's face between her soft hands.

"See? See?" She sobbed while staring into his face with a terrified expression. "Who was that, huh? What do they want? Your ass should have stayed in school. You ain't built for this life!"

Her words were drowned out because suddenly there was a loud scream from behind the counter. Boogie pulled away from his mother to go see what had happened. His feet crunched on shattered glass as he went to look over the counter, and he almost wished he hadn't. Three employees were kneeling beside another, who was bleeding out at the neck.

"Gia." Boogie's voice was just above a whisper.

She had a hand pressed to the wound on her neck, but blood was seeping through her fingers. Boogie could see her hand growing weaker, and she lay there choking on her own blood. Her eyes fell on him, and they spoke to him. She was begging him to help her, but there was nothing he could do. She tried to talk through her stained-red teeth, but the only thing that came out was a bunch of gargled nothings.

"Dina, get out of here. I'll handle it," Boogie heard Caesar say to his mother behind him.

"But—"

"I said go! You don't need to be here."

Boogie turned around to see her stepping through the shot-out glass door of the establishment. She looked back again at the scene before holding a hand to her chest and hurrying away. Caesar went around the counter and saw what Boogie was looking at. When he saw, his expression didn't change.

"We have to help her," Boogie told him.

"She's already dead," Caesar said and turned to the three women sobbing around Gia's body. "Quickly, one of you, I need the recordings from inside and outside of this building."

"Th . . . the cameras don't work right now," the oldest of them said. Her name tag said DEBBIE, and she looked to be in her early forties. "Barry was in the middle of getting a new security system installed when he died."

"Show me," Caesar told her.

Debbie nodded and took Caesar to the back of the business. After a few minutes, the two of them reemerged, and Boogie assumed that Debbie had been telling the truth. Caesar gave each woman a stare that was so chilling even Boogie felt the coldness from it.

"We were never here, understand?"

"Yes, Caesar," all of them answered in unison.

"You will each be compensated for what you saw today and for your cooperation. You know what happens to people with loose lips. Let's go, Boogie."

He walked calmly to the exit, and Boogie took one last glance at Gia lying in a pool of her own blood staring emptily at the ceiling. Caesar was right. There was nothing that he could do. He gritted his teeth and pushed off the counter before following Caesar into his vehicle.

"That was your boy, wasn't it?"

"Yeah, that was Shane. That nigga just tried to kill me."

"No," Caesar disagreed. "That was a warning. He was letting you know that he's back in your city. Now the question is, what are you gon' do about it?"

Chapter 9

Against his suggestion, Boogie made Caesar take him to his own car. He couldn't move around the way he wanted to riding passenger. He needed to be behind his own wheels. The two men made plans to meet up later that day to run down the next play, but first Boogie had some things to check up on. Bentley was the first person Boogie called once he was alone in his own car.

"Bro, I was just about to hit you. You good?" Bentley asked as soon as he answered. "Some niggas just let off on me in traffic. I had to hop out the whip and make a break for it."

"Fuck. Where you at right now?"

"On the way to the crib."

"Okay. Watch yourself. It was Shane who did that to you."

"How you know?"

"Because he just hit my pop's cleaning business. He killed one of the employees tryin'a make some noise."

"Tryin'a make some noise? That nigga is pretty loud to me. That nigga is gon' keep tryin'a kill us if we don't come up with a way to get him first," Bentley told him.

"I know. Fuck!" Boogie hit the steering wheel. "I knew we should have never gone on that hit in the first place. Now I have this crazy motherfucka on my dick. Too much is goin' on at once. This shit is stupid."

"Word. But you ain't alone in it. We just gotta tighten up on our end. Drastically. Bro, where you at?"

"In traffic right now. You need me to come grab you?"

"Yeah. I need to go check on my sister and the baby. She supposed to be at my crib, but she ain't answering the phone."

"You think Shane know where you stay?"

"I don't know. But you know money talks around Brooklyn. Give the right motherfucka a dollar and they'll be singing like a bird. I'm over here by that old laundromat that burned down. By Bed-Stuy."

"A'ight, stay there. I'm about to pull up on you."

Boogie hung up and put his car in drive. All he could think about was Roz and Amber. He just hoped they were okay. It took him thirty minutes to get to Bentley and another fifteen to get to Bentley's apartment.

"There her car go," Bentley said, pointing at a Honda Civic that was double-parked in the apartment parking lot. "Why the fuck she ain't answerin' the phone? If he did somethin' to my sister or my niece, there will be hell to pay!"

The two of them hopped out of the car and hurried inside of the complex. Bentley ran up the stairs first, and Boogie wasn't too far behind him. He paid attention to his surroundings just in case something unexpected planned to pop out and surprise him. However, the coast seemed clear. Still, Boogie rested his hand over the gun at his waist.

"Roz!" Bentley called when he burst through the door of his place. "Roz! You here?"

"Shhh!" Roz exclaimed, rushing from the back bedroom folding a baby towel. "I just put Amber to sleep."

She was wearing a pair of formfitting jeans and a white tank top. Her hair had been scooped up into a bun on top of her head, and a colorful bandana was wrapped around her edges. She gave her brother a bewildered look like she was wondering why he was making so much noise.

"Yo, why the fuck weren't you answerin' the phone?" Bentley exclaimed, ignoring what she'd just said. "I called you like ten times!"

"I was putting Amber to sleep. My phone was on silent," she said, and she took notice of Boogie standing by the front door. "Is everything okay?"

"Hell nah! Some niggas just tried to kill me! I had to leave my car in traffic."

"Wasn't it stolen anyways?"

"That's beside the point! What needs to happen now is that you need to grab Amb and get all your shit together so we can go."

"They know where you live?"

"Shit, I don't know. But if they spotted me out in a stolen vehicle, I don't know what else they can find out."

"But—"

"Roz, we gotta go," Boogie finally stepped in. He went to the patio window to peer down into the parking lot. He didn't see anything suspicious, but still he wanted to be safe instead of sorry. "We don't know how much time we have."

"Okay." Roz gave an annoyed sighed. "Let me get all my shit so I can be wrapped up in y'all's shit. I don't even know if I want to ask."

"Don't," both Boogie and Bentley said at the same time.

The annoyed look on her face quickly turned into one of concern. She placed the towel in her hands on her shoulder and looked back and forth between the two of them. Slowly one hand went to her waist, and the other had a finger pointed in their direction.

"Does this have something to do with all that money you brought in here the other day? And don't you lie to me, Bentley!"

"He'll explain everything to you once we're safe and sound at my condo," Boogie told her.

"I wasn't talking to you." Roz cut her eyes at him and turned her attention back to her brother. "Now what's going on?"

"It does have something to do with the money," Bentley admitted with a sigh. "The person we took it from has the kind of beef that usually ends with somebody dead. They already got at Boogie, and they just tried to get at me. That's why we have to leave right now, because if something happens to you or my niece, the whole borough of Brooklyn will pay for it. Now get your things and come on!"

His words must have gotten to her, because the next thing they knew, Roz was hurrying to the back room and gathering anything she could carry. When she reappeared, she had a sleeping Amber, a diaper bag, and a duffle bag that she dropped at her brother's feet. He picked it up and unzipped it, revealing a heap of cash inside.

"I thought you'd want that since it is the reason we're in this mess," she said tersely.

Bentley didn't dignify the statement with a response and instead zipped the bag up again. Before they left, he went into his bedroom, and when he came out, he had a backpack filled with things he needed. He nodded at Boogie, letting him know that he was ready, and the four of them left the apartment. Once outside, Bentley opted to follow Boogie to his home in Roz's car with her.

Boogie didn't remember a time when he was more paranoid. Every five seconds he found himself glancing in his rearview mirror to make sure nobody was following them. He even took the long way and a few extra turns to get to his place. When they finally arrived, he instructed Roz to park in his guest parking space beside his. By the time they got inside his condo, Boogie felt his paranoia subside a little bit.

"Roz, you and the baby can stay in my guest room," he said and pointed her down the hallway. "Bentley, dog, the living room has a pullout if that's coo' with you."

"That's a'ight with me," Bentley said, looking around Boogie's setup. "Yo' crib is nice. It's most def time for me to upgrade."

"Do whatever is right for you, bro," Boogie said and plopped down on one of his couches. "I just got this spot because it wasn't too far from my school. But now none of that shit matters anymore. Not when that Shane and his daddy are after us. I still can't believe them niggas got to dumpin' at the cleaners like that. In broad daylight."

"Well, believe it. They want us bad. We gotta make some shit shake."

"On me," Boogie agreed. "Speakin' of which, I gotta call Caesar and see what time he wants to link up later."

"Hold up," Bentley said, sitting down on the recliner diagonally across from where Boogie was sitting. "When you start hangin' with Caesar?"

"Since my old man got killed."

"Y'all puttin' your heads together to try to figure out who did him in?"

"That, and I'm supposed to take his place."

"Duh, nigga. I mean, everything your dad left behind is rightfully yours."

"Everything except his seat with the heads of the Five Families. The other four have to vote me in."

"So what, Caesar's doin' some type of initiation or some shit?"

"Man, I don't know what the fuck he's doin', but he's definitely testin' my temperature. I really don't know what's up now since this Shane and Shamar shit. Caesar was with me when they hit the cleaners. He asked me what I was gon' do about it."

"You know what I'm thinkin'?"

"What?"

"You need that seat at that table. And I'll be your right-hand man. We already waist deep in this thing together. We ain't close, but you my nigga. I mean, I didn't try to kill you when I found out you made a move on my sister without getting my blessing first."

Boogie's head whipped toward Bentley, whose eye-brow was raised. Boogie looked sheepishly at him.

"Yeah, she told me about y'all's little date. Don't un-derestimate how close she and I are. We tell each other everything. She and my niece are the only people in the world I care about."

"Yo, my bad on that. I wasn't even thinkin'."

"You was thinkin', just not with the right head. If I didn't think Roz could handle herself, I woulda deaded that. But you gon' see that for yourself." Bentley shrugged, leav-ing Boogie to wonder what exactly he was talking about. "Back to the real shit we got on the table. You do know what Caesar is wantin', right?"

"No." Boogie shook his head.

"A'ight, how much does he know about our involve-ment with the hit on Shane?"

"Everything."

"He know who Shane is?"

"Yup."

"And has he said anything about it to the other four Families?"

"Nah. I don't think so anyway," Boogie answered. "He might have though."

"I doubt he said anything. That motherfucka Caesar is a fuckin' titan. If he wanted Shane and Shamar dead, they would be. No question. He wants you to handle it. I think he wants you to clean up your own mess. This is your ticket to the cool table. So, are you gon' cash in or what?"

Boogie let his words set in. He felt like Bentley was right. He thought back to how calm Caesar was after the shooting earlier that day. He didn't budge or make any phone calls of his own. He even let Boogie venture off on his own after something crazy like that had just occurred. Boogie knew it was on him. It was time to grow up and become the man Barry had always wanted him to be.

"We need a plan," Boogie said. "I need to know where they're hidin' out at. I know he wouldn't be dumb enough to go back to that same condo. That spot is too hot."

"Already on it," Bentley said, standing. "I'ma check in with you in a few hours."

He grabbed Roz's keys off the counter and was out the door in seconds. Boogie trusted that he would come back with something. One thing he'd learned about Bentley by working with him was that he always had his ear to the streets. It had proven to be useful when they would go on their hits, and Boogie hoped it would prove to be useful then.

Upon hearing the front door shut, Roz ventured back down the hallway. She glanced around the living room first, and when she didn't see her brother, she glanced at the counter in the kitchen. Seeing that her keys weren't there, she rolled her eyes. "Don't y'all got people after y'all? Why is it so hard for my brother to stay put?"

"You can only do that in this life for so long," Boogie told her, taking his shoes off and kicking his feet up on the couch. "When the streets move, you gotta move too."

"Well, why ain't it you out there in the field instead of him?"

"Because Bentley is doin' what Bentley does best right now."

"And that is?"

"Gatherin' information. You should know your brother better than anybody. And you know it's true when I say that he can find out anything he wants to know."

"Mmm," Roz said, but she didn't refute that. She looked him up and down and smacked her lips. "Why are you even in the streets anyway? Ain't you tryin'a be a chef or something like that?"

"That's what I wanted to do, yeah. But things change. People change, too," he said, looking into her face. "What you think you know about me anyway?"

"Only what my brother tells me."

"And what is that?"

Before Roz answered him, she came over to the couch he was lying back on and pushed his legs toward the back cushions so that she could sit down. Her pretty eyes traveled from his lips to his nose and then finally up to his brown eyes. Once again Boogie took in her beauty. That time, he noticed she had a tiny mole right next to her nose. It gave her face character, and he liked it.

She said, "He said you're one of the smartest men he's ever worked with, and you're about your paper. That you're a good leader, but your heart ain't in the game. And that's something that can get you killed."

"I'd have to agree with all of that."

"Well, if your heart ain't in the game, what you in it for?"

"Just because I didn't choose the game never meant that it wouldn't choose me," Boogie said with a shrug, and then he sighed. "You know, when my dad was here, I don't think I ever appreciated the red carpet he laid out for me. I was too busy tryin'a run from it."

"Why? Hell, I wish we came from some money. It wasn't until Bentley started working for Barry that our lives turned around."

"I don't know. I just spent so long tryin'a run from it that I never even asked myself why. I just thought I didn't want the life my pops wanted for me. But look where I landed. Maybe my heart wasn't always in it, but it's here now. Because now that my pops is gone, all I want to do is continue his legacy. I'll do anything to ensure that."

"Are you built for that?"

"'You recreate yourself for the life you want.'"

"Huh?"

"That's what my pops always said. I guess he just meant that you adapt when it comes to the things you want. And I want a seat at that table."

"I like that," Roz said with a half-smile. "And I believe in you. Hell, I have to. Because you still owe me a date, and a dead man can't take me to Ruth's Chris."

Boogie went to say something else, but there was a sudden cry of a fussy baby from the guest bedroom. She stood up with a wink before she went to go check on Amber. As she walked away, Boogie smirked to himself before reaching for his phone to call Caesar.

Caesar sat alone in the study of his home puffing on a Cuban cigar. Normally after a fiasco like the one that happened at the cleaners, Caesar would have found the culprits and had their heads severed from their bodies. But he didn't. Even though Shane and Shamar had moved in on his business, and even had collected a nice amount of change while doing so under his nose, he still didn't think it was fitting for him to do away with them. Mainly that was because he knew that he could, and it would be too easy. Within five minutes of taking Boogie home, Caesar found out that Shane and Shamar were lying low in an apartment in Bushwick. He could have had the unit stormed and everyone in it slaughtered, but Caesar recognized that, for once, it was not his fight. Boogie had to find his own footing in the game, just like he and Barry had.

Caesar glanced down in his lap at the photo book he'd been glancing through. It was an old one, one that hadn't been pulled out in ages. It was open to a page with a photo of two young men sitting on an old-school Cutlass. Each had an arm around each other and a small smile. Caesar had almost laughed when he saw how big his and Barry's afros had been back in the day. Back then they weren't just colleagues. They were best friends, thick as thieves, even while the Families were feuding. Barry had been the one who helped Caesar sort through the loss of both of his parents, and Caesar had been the best man at Barry's wedding. Their falling out was something that was inevitable, but something that could have been prevented at the same time. Caesar reflected on the day that changed their friendship forever.

"Negro, I can't believe you pulled up here in another new car! You better quit, or Dina is gon' want one of these motherfuckas!"

Caesar grinned as he stepped out of his new Mustang in Barry's driveway. The two men slapped hands and embraced. Caesar had just gotten back from doing a business deal with the Italians, and he was excited to run it by Barry. It was something he knew the other table members wouldn't understand, but he knew Barry would have his back.

"Man, if you don't break down and buy that woman a new car . . . You got the money for it."

"Yeah, yeah." Barry waved Caesar's words away. "The only car that woman needs is a van to drive my little man around."

"Where is my godson by the way?"

"Where he always is: in the house on his mama's hip. I can't wait until he's older so I can show him the ropes of the family business. Come on in. I know you said you have something important to tell me about."

Barry led Caesar into the spacious home he'd purchased with his wife. The moment Caesar stepped in, he smelled something delicious coming from the kitchen. He was glad to know that that was the direction they were going in, because he hadn't eaten anything on the way back from Staten Island. As soon as they got to the kitchen, his stomach growled loudly, and Barry laughed.

"Hold your horses, hungry man. Dina made some of her famous chili. Ain't that right, baby?" Barry said to his wife, who was standing in front of the stove.

"That's right," Dina said and grinned at her husband. Sure enough, she was standing there with their son attached to her hip as she stirred a big pot of chili. Boogie grinned at Caesar, who couldn't resist going over and taking him from his mother.

"Girl, give me this baby before you burn him," he joked.

"Uh-uh, Caesar. Don't do me like that. Boogie likes being with his mama while she cooks. That boy might be a chef one day."

"Not if I have my way with him," Barry commented and went to sit at one of the high chairs at the kitchen island.

"Yeah, yeah," Dina said, shaking her head and causing her big hair to bounce. "I'll make y'all some bowls real quick so you can talk business."

Caesar played with his 1-year-old godson while she did that. He couldn't believe how big he'd gotten, but they always said kids grow up fast. Boogie might not have been his kid biologically, but Caesar loved the boy, and he took the godfather role seriously. When Boogie was born, Caesar vowed to Barry that if anything were to ever happen to him, he would have nothing to worry about.

When Dina set their food on the island, Caesar gave Boogie a kiss on the forehead and handed him back to his mother.

"You look good with kids, Caesar. When are you gon' have some of your own?"

"Whenever God allows it. Right now, Boogie is all the baby I need."

"Uh-huh. Well, I hope you're strapping up. You know all these little hoochies are after you and your li'l money."

"Now, Dina, you know ain't nothing little about my money."

"Exactly," she said, giving him a knowing look before leaving the kitchen.

"She is something else," Caesar said, sitting down on a stool beside Barry.

"I know. That's why I married her," Barry said. "Now what was so urgent that you couldn't tell me over the telephone and had to be said in person?" He took a big bite of his chili and waited for Caesar to respond.

Before he did, Caesar too had to take some big bites of food to settle the noise that his stomach was still making. When his bowl was half gone, he wiped his mouth on a napkin and smiled big. "I did something today that nobody thought would be possible."

"And that is?"

"Expanded."

"Nigga, we always knew you were capable of expanding. The market is hot right now."

"Well, it will be even hotter once I expand to Staten Island," Caesar said, and Barry stopped chewing.

"Staten Island?" he asked as if to make sure he'd heard correctly. *"Ain't that the Italians' territory?"*

"I just left from seeing Bosco," Caesar said, nodding. *"We talked business, and he's willing to discuss his options about joining the table."*

"Joining the table? As in the Five Families?"

"Yeah, but it would of course be changed to the Six Families. Like it was supposed to be."

"But Bosco turned the Pact down," Barry reminded him. *"He didn't want anything to do with us or our territories. What's changed?"*

"Well, that's changed now that I told him that if he joins the table, he would be able to conduct business in all the territories."

"You what?" Barry asked and looked at Caesar as if he had lost his mind. *"Do you want another war to break out?"*

"It won't as long as everybody knows their place," Caesar explained. *"He would only have certain areas where he'd be able to do his business, so you and the other Families would still control the capital. And in turn, I get to expand my drug business into Staten Island."*

"Only you?"

"For now, yes," Caesar answered, and Barry scoffed.

"Unbelievable. So, you're basically making a decision that affects all of us but only suits your needs."

"I'm looking at the bigger picture. Bosco has the kinds of connects I need, and if I eat, everybody eats. When

I win, everybody wins. You of all people know this, Barry."

"You don't have the power or authority to make a decision like this, Caesar. You know there would have to be a vote, and I can already tell you with whom the other Families are going to side."

"And that's why I need you to side with me, old friend. If they see that you back my decision, they'll have no choice but to give it a chance. Everyone thinks you're the sensible one."

"That's because I am," Barry said and then looked at Caesar with stern eyes. "And that's why I'm going to tell you that this makes no sense. And I don't trust Bosco for one minute. If you give him an inch, he'll figure out a way to take ten miles. There is a reason he never wanted to be part of the Pact in the first place. He doesn't follow anybody's rules but his own. You know this."

"So, you're saying I won't be able to count on your vote?"

"I'm saying I'm going to give the other Family leaders a heads-up on the fact that you've been going behind their backs, bartering their territories for personal gain. And we all know what that will lead to. Unless you drop this mess altogether and tell Bosco that the deal is off. You'll just have to find your connects somewhere else."

The two men had a stare down. Caesar felt an anger and betrayal that he'd never experienced before brewing inside of him. He didn't understand why Barry didn't have his back on the topic. But the one thing he wouldn't do was beg. Caesar knew without that vote that the others would never go for it, and Caesar's loyalty to them ran too deep to allow Bosco to join the table *without their consent. He was stuck, and being stuck was a feeling he hated. The air around the two men had shifted, maybe forever. Caesar's pride wouldn't allow him to look at Barry as his greatest friend anymore.*

When he left, he didn't even say goodbye to Dina and the baby.

Caesar blinked out of his memory and sighed deeply. That memory was his greatest regret, because after that day, the dynamic of their relationship did change. Not on Barry's part, but on Caesar's. Barry tried time and time again to make things right with Caesar, but in Caesar's mind, Barry had made it very clear that there was a thin line between friendship and business. So, Caesar had opted to stay on the business side all the way up until Barry's death.

Because of his stubborn behavior, Caesar never got the opportunity to have his friend back. That was why it was so important to him to figure out who was behind his death. It also was why Caesar felt it was his duty to honor his promise to Barry as the godfather of his child. He hadn't brought up the issue of Shamar Hafford to the other Families. At first he felt that it wasn't their business to know, but he soon came to realize he didn't want anything to get in the way of Boogie's destiny. If he were to tell the others what had transpired, they would see Boogie as a reckless kid, but Caesar was coming to learn that he was more than that. Much more.

Boogie had impressed him more than Caesar thought he would when he had him ride around with him. He reminded him of Barry, except Boogie was his own person with his own mind. Caesar could tell that the world hadn't turned the boy's heart into stone yet, not even through his father's death. It was a trait that even he had to admit the table needed. Still, he wasn't sure if Boogie was ready to fill his father's seat yet. He had to see how he handled the situation with Shane and Shamar before he could make a decision, so he hoped the situation would be taken care of before the vote happened.

Beside him on the table next to his chair, Caesar's phone began to vibrate. It didn't catch him off guard because he had been expecting the call, although it was from an unknown number. "Did you find what I was looking for?" Caesar said when he answered.

"Yes," a man's voice said on the other end of the phone. "I'm outside your front door."

"Perfect," Caesar said and disconnected the call.

Whoever had murdered Barry had covered their tracks so well that none of Caesar's men had been able to pick up a trail. It forced Caesar to go to plan B. He hired a private investigator. Normally he didn't work with the law, but Douglas was his cousin and someone who didn't mind accepting money under the table. It helped that they had different last names and nobody ever made the connection. It helped having a mole who could access any security camera in the state whenever he needed it. Caesar had given him all of the places that Barry frequented, his low-key spots, and also the places he'd gone that day in hopes that Douglas could pick up a trace of what had happened. He was one of the best in his field if one were to let him tell it. And Caesar had to admit that he was worth the money.

Caesar closed the photo book on his lap and placed it on the floor. He then grabbed an envelope of cash from the drawer in the table before he got up to make his way to the front door of his mansion. When he reached the foyer, his two full-grown Cane Corso dogs were already at the door. They could sense that someone was on the other side. He told them to sit, and when he opened the door, there was Douglas in a black hoodie holding a thick yellow folder in his hands. Caesar stepped out of the way so that he could enter, but Douglas shook his head.

"Not with those monsters looking like they want to take a bite out of me. I already almost got a bullet put in my head from your security before I told them my name. Plus, I'm working on another case. I need to get home," he said. "I just wanted to personally deliver this to you and say . . ."

"Say what?"

"Prepare yourself for what you're about to see in there. It's not pretty. But you'll have your answer."

With that, the two men exchanged packages, and Douglas was gone. Caesar shut the door to his home and stared at the folder to his hands. Slowly and with his dogs at his feet, he made his way back to his study and tried to mentally prepare himself for what he was about to see. He sat back down and took a deep breath before he opened the folder and poured its many contents on his lap.

There were documents and text conversations between Barry and many of his associates. Caesar sifted through them but didn't find anything he was looking for in them. He moved on to the photos and realized that Barry frequented Diana's club more often than he thought. He found himself smirking. Caesar knew Barry loved his wife, but there was just something about getting new and different pussy every now and then that kept him young. Caesar sorted through a few more photos before he came across one that made him freeze. He studied it and looked at another photo behind it . . . and then another. He felt as if he'd just swallowed a ton of bricks. Douglas was right. He did know now who had murdered Barry.

The sound of his phone ringing from his pocket was the only thing that was able to force his eyes away from the photographs. Slowly he pulled the device out and answered it once he saw that it was Boogie calling him. In his momentary shock, he forgot the two of them were supposed to be meeting back up later that day.

"Boogie, everything good?" Caesar asked when he answered.

"Yeah, everything is straight. So, what's the play?"

"About that," Caesar said, looking back down at the photos in his lap. "You'll have to handle that on your own."

"Wait, you ain't rollin' with me?"

"I can't. Something came up."

"Somethin' came up?" Boogie asked as if he hadn't heard Caesar correctly.

"Exactly," Caesar answered. He didn't mean to sound so disinterested, but his mind was elsewhere. "Get them out of your city, and make sure they never do business in our territories again. If you can do that, your father's seat is as good as yours. I'll make sure the others know that you're ready to take on the job."

"What? Caesar, you seen how them niggas came at me at the cleaners. Shit, they came at you too! How am I supposed to go against that by myself?"

"The same way you got into this situation."

"So, you ain't gon' help me like you said, and you still haven't found out who killed my pop? Had me rollin' with you and do all that shit that ain't have nothin' to do with me, but you can't even watch my back. Like you said, I'm not mobbed up!"

"I said that to see what you would believe," Caesar told him. "You're too naive, kid. Get rid of that trait. We're Five what?"

"Families. But what that gotta do with you not pullin' up?"

"You just said it. Majority of the people working under Barry are your family. Do you think they'll let you go into a war alone?"

"Man, whatever."

"Boogie—"

"Nah, it's coo'. Don't worry, I got it."

Caesar didn't bother trying to stop him because he knew what was next. He removed the phone from his ear before he heard the click of the other end hanging up. If he were Boogie, he would be upset too by the brush-off. That was the only reason Caesar was going to let him get away with hanging up in his face. If Boogie was anything like his old man, he would figure things out with Shane and Shamar. Hopefully he would also still have his life when it was all said and done. As much as he wanted to be the one to snap Shamar's neck for moving in on New York's drug trade, Caesar had to figure out what the photos really meant.

Chapter 10

Boogie wanted nothing more than to throw his phone down and shout curses into the universe, but he didn't want to alarm Roz any more than he and Bentley already had. It was bad enough that she was inadvertently involved in their mess in the first place.

He couldn't believe that Caesar had played him. He didn't know if he was so angry because Caesar had gone back on his word or because, after the few days he'd spent with him, he was starting to like the man. Instead of blanking out on everything around him, Boogie paced his home for hours trying to come up with a game plan. He couldn't give Shane another chance to get at him. The next time the two saw each other would have to be on his terms.

Just as he was just starting to form a plan, there was a knock at his front door. The loud banging jarred him out of his deep thought and made him instinctively grab for the Beretta he kept strapped to the bottom of his kitchen island. Cocking it, he slowly advanced to the door and glanced out the peephole.

"Damn," he said to himself, seeing that it was only Bentley.

His paranoia was getting the best of him. Before he had checked to see who it was, half of him had wanted to open the door and just get to blasting. He was glad he didn't. He would have forever regretted it. Unlocking the door, Boogie swung it open and let Bentley inside.

"My bad it took me so long, Boog—" Bentley stopped midsentence, seeing the gun in Boogie's hand. "Everything straight, G?"

"Yeah. Just takin' extra precautions," Boogie said and let the door shut. After locking it, he walked back into the kitchen and set the weapon down on a counter. "You find out anything?"

"I gotta pour up for this," Bentley answered, shaking his head. "What you got to drink?"

"All dark," Boogie told him, grabbing two glasses down from his cabinet.

"Some Crown is good with me."

Boogie nodded and poured them both a shot before handing Bentley a glass. Boogie wasted no time throwing his back. A hiss escaped his lips as the burning sensation of the liquid making its way down his throat hit him. They set their empty glasses down at the same time and looked at each other.

Bentley shook his head. "Have I ever told you about my cousin Gino?"

"Nah. He with one of the Families?"

"Nah. He's one of those niggas who never picked a side. He never liked being told when, what, and why. Gino is somethin' of a floater. He lives all over the state of New York. Well, right now his place of choice is Brooklyn. Bushwick to be exact."

"And what about it?"

"A'ight, check this. Gino runs what I'll just call a gun trade from his apartment."

"He must work with Marco in Queens."

"Didn't you just hear me say that he ain't part of any of the Families like me and you? He works for himself."

"What? He couldn't have pulled off no shit like that without my pop knowin' about it."

"And Barry would have known if Gino did business with folks from New York, but he doesn't. The only way his business can work is if he does business with niggas from out of town. If they have a gun they need to get rid of when shit is real hot, they bring it to him and get a new one. Some niggas just come looking for upgrades. Either way, he's makin' that bread."

"So, what does this have to do with Shane and Shamar?"

"I'm getting to that part, impatient nigga."

"My bad."

"It's cool, but listen up. I just left Gino's spot, and guess what he tells me. That some niggas from Ohio came to see him this morning. They needed some Ks to handle some chump nigga."

"And let me guess, I was the chump nigga?" Boogie asked.

"Yup, but don't take it personal."

"I'm not. But I'm tryin' hard not to blank at the fact that your cousin sold these niggas the weapons they used to almost kill me."

"Chill out. It was an honest mistake. He ain't know they were after Barry Tolliver's son. But you gotta look at the bigger picture, son."

"And that is?"

"Gino said they're lyin' low in an apartment complex near him. And for the right price, I bet he can find out exactly what unit and get us in there to handle our business."

"Fuck the price. That was already paid by him making money in Brooklyn and not payin' his dues. He gon' tell me whatever it is I want to know. Make the call."

Thick puffs of smoke carried the scent of marijuana all throughout a compact one-room apartment. One man sat casually on a futon in the bedroom turned office. A thick cigar filled with the best weed New York had to offer rested between the thumb and the pointer finger of his right hand. As relaxed as he was, one might not have believed the horrendous act that was taking place in front of him. His left hand played with a ring on one of his fingers, twisting it every so often as he watched his goons beat a man blue to black. The man looked toward him, with blood leaking from a gash underneath his left eye.

"Gino, bro. C'mon! I—" His shaky plea was cut short by four hard knuckles connecting with his mouth.

Gino watched him fly back and held a hand up to his goons. They'd done enough for the moment. He took a long draft from the blunt and exhaled before exercising his vocal cords.

"Cordell, you've disappointed me. You know that, right?" Gino said, shaking his head. "I don't tend to trust many niggas, but I almost trusted you. Did you really think you would get away with stealin' from me? Did you think that I wouldn't find out that I have ten guns missing with no payment for them?"

Cordell proved that disloyalty had no designated look. He was tall and goofy, always the class clown back when they had gone to school together. Gino thought he would be a good addition to his team, being that he had the lips that could sell ice to a polar bear. Things were going good until almost a year in when Gino, who was very hands-on with his own accounting, began noticing numbers and inventory not adding up. It took almost a month to snuff out who was back-alley selling his tradable weapons. And when he did, he vowed that Cordell would pay the price.

"I was gon' get you your money, Gino. You gotta believe me. Please. You gotta believe me."

"I don't give a fuck about what you're talkin' about. The money should have been in my pocket before my shit left my possession."

"I . . . I'll get you your money, Gino. I swear!"

"You played a dangerous game, Cordell. What you don't understand is that I'm already used to not having that money, so you'll have to pay me back in another way."

"Anything."

"Fifteen guns? I need fifteen souls. Until your debt is paid, you're out of the office and on the streets. And if you even think about doin' somethin' stupid, just remember that pretty little girl of yours, Malia. And her mother, Melissa. Hell, think about your own mother, Cora, and your grandma."

"Don't hurt them."

"Then make sure you do as I say," Gino said and motioned for one of the goons to take him out of his office.

The remaining man in the office gave Gino a funny look as he put his blunt out. "You sure you don't want me to knock that nigga off, G?"

The goon was a young, dark-skinned man who Gino had given the name Bic because his temper came as quick as flicking a lighter. He was no more than 20 years old, though his deep voice gave the illusion that he was much older. Bic had the "get money" mentality that Gino liked, and he was also loyal, like a dog almost. Gino could always depend on him to be at his heels. He was always on go and as good with his fists as he was with a pistol.

"Leave him," Gino said, leaning back into the futon.

"I don't mean to question your judgment, but that nigga already proved that he was disloyal to the family. How do we know that he won't go runnin' his mouth about your whole operation and have that motherfucka Marco at your door?"

"He won't. Cordell is a family man. He'll do anything to protect them. Plus, now that I know it was him who went against me, he'll be watched like a hawk, until his debt is paid anyway. Then I won't have any use for him anymore."

Knock! Knock!

The loud sound of the front door banging traveled to the back room, and shortly after, one of the men Gino had standing guard in the front room was standing in the office's doorway. The Mac 11 he toted hung at his side, and he pointed a thumb behind him.

"Ay, boss, your cousin is here again. He got another nigga with him this time."

Gino sighed and fixed the collar of his striped button-up. "I told that nigga Bentley about bringin' people I don't know up in here."

Although Bentley was his first cousin, Gino still grabbed his piece from his desk. He trusted Bentley with his life, but being strapped was a habit. He motioned his head for his soldier to move out of his way so he could go to the front. Bentley had just left from his spot a couple hours prior after asking him questions about a few men he'd sold some guns to. At first Gino wanted to know what business his cousin had with a kingpin and his son, but when he thought better of it, he didn't want to know anything.

When Gino rounded the corner, he instantly spotted his cousin standing in the middle of the front room next to a man with a familiar face. The only thing was that Gino knew he had never met him a day in his life, so he couldn't figure out why he felt like he'd met him before.

"Cuz, what you doin' back this way?"

"I just had to come rap to you real quick," Bentley said and slapped hands with Gino.

"I thought you just did that," Gino said to Bentley but was eyeing the man in the gray sweat suit standing next to him. He didn't like the look being aimed his way. In fact, it made the hairs on the back of his neck stand up. "You got a problem, fam?"

"Yeah, you."

"Yo, Boogie. Chill out. You said you were gon' be coo'."

"Hell nah. This the nigga responsible for the hit on my pop's business. Give me one reason why I shouldn't off this motherfucka right now."

Gino held up a hand to stop his men from surrounding Boogie. He either had to be stupid or really bold to come up into his place of business talking recklessly. Gino had to admit, he was curious to know which.

"I sell guns to a lot of men, men who are gettin' guns to—I don't know, hmm, let me see—use them?" Gino said, and the men standing around him chuckled. "I don't keep track of where the weapons go once the money is in my hands. Now, Bentley, who the fuck is this nigga you got in my spot talkin' greasy to me?"

"I'm right here, so talk to me," Boogie spoke, and the bass in his voice made Gino give him eye contact.

"Fine. Who the fuck are you?"

"The nigga whose territory you're in doin' business you ain't got no business doin'."

"Ha!" Gino gave a forced laugh. "Last I checked, this was Barry Tolliver's territory, and if I'm not mistaken, he's dead."

"It was Barry Tolliver's territory. Now it's his son's."

"You're Barry's son?" Gino asked, eyeing Boogie even though he already knew the answer. That was why Boogie looked so familiar. He resembled his father so much it was like Barry's presence was in the room with them. Truth be told, it wasn't Marco finding out about Gino's business that made him wary. It had always been Barry. He would have sent Gino home to his mother's house cut up in a trash bag if he had discovered what he was doing there. And that was the biggest reason Gino only did business with out-of-towners: they were people who had no connection to New York besides him.

"You know the answer to that," Boogie said. "What I'm tryin'a figure out is, if you're in my city, how are you workin' and I never gave you a job?"

Boogie looked at all the polished weapons sitting out on a coffee table and at the men standing around. Gino clenched his jaw and glared at him. In seconds, the nobody who had come in with his cousin had been revealed to be the boss. As much as he wanted to tell his soldiers to light Boogie up, he knew all hell would rain down on him if he did so. Gino glared at his cousin for blowing up his spot.

"Don't look at him like that, fam. In all honesty, he's the reason I didn't come in here guns blazin'."

"Is that right?"

"Dead ass. Plus, you have information that I need."

"Information like what?"

"Like where the men you sold those Ks to are hiding."

"Hmm, interesting," Gino said, tapping his chin. "What are you willing to pay for that info?"

"I'm willin' to walk out of here and let you keep your life," Boogie offered.

Gino studied his face and, in seconds, could tell that Boogie was serious. Keeping his same composure, Gino laughed, not wanting to let Boogie know the emptiness in his eyes made Gino want to step back. Boogie had the look of a man who had nothing to lose, which was even more dangerous, because as the head of Brooklyn, he had everything to lose.

"A'ight," Gino sighed. "You run a tough bargain. So, I'll tell you what I want to know. A little broad named Stephanie brought Shane to me. Said her dude needed to grab a few things from me. I could tell he was big time, and when I found out who he really was, I let him off the strength of Stephanie's connection to Diana. I ain't think she was on no foul type of time. Plus, his money talked loudly. Shane is stayin' with her in that apartment complex down the street. The one with the flickering lights."

"And how you know he stayin' with her?"

"I notice every movement around here. And to anybody else, the niggas standin' out there just look like they're standin' around. But I know shooters when I see them. And shooters wouldn't be standin' outside if he weren't inside."

"How we know you tellin' the truth about how you know him? How we know you ain't the one he checks in with when he touches down?" Boogie speculated.

"Me?" Gino looked appalled. "Hell nah, you got that shit wrong. It was bad enough havin' to look out for

Barry, but you think I want Caesar sniffing down my back too? I know there's only one reason a cat like Shane could be in New York. He bought his guns from me, that's all. I have no part in anything else he does. And I only know where Stephanie lives because shorty gets around, if you know what I mean. Now I gave you all the information you need. Is there anything else?"

"Besides me tellin' you that you have to shut down shop or move it to Queens? Cousin of Bentley's or not, he chose a family to work for, so it's time for you to choose too. If you want to continue making money in this state anyway."

Gino wanted to say something else, but Boogie had already turned to leave. They had gotten all the information that they needed out of him. Boogie went out first, but Bentley hung back, and Gino gave him a hard glare.

"Yo, what the fuck were you thinkin' bringin' that nigga in my spot?" he asked.

"Look, I ain't think he was gon' go crazy on you like that. But you forced his hand with all that rah-rah you was talking. Be grateful all he's makin' you do is switch locations. Just stay by your phone, a'ight, cuz? I might need your services later."

"And you think I'ma just say yeah like that? After you just blew up my spot?"

"Yeah, I do, if you want to be plugged in directly with Marco. Them niggas in Queens are makin' triple what you are doin' the same shit. Be on go when I say, and I'll make sure you and your whole team eats. Coo'?"

"I don't know," Gino said, outwardly still angry at Bentley. What he had put on the table was an appetizing offer though, and he couldn't deny that. More money was always the goal. "I'll think about it."

"Look, just answer the phone when I call. I'm out." Bentley threw up two fingers and left Gino to ponder what he'd said.

"Yo, nigga. Why you go in there on all that 'Big Boss Nigga' shit?" Bentley asked once he was back in the car with Boogie. "I ain't never seen my cousin shook like that."

"I wanted to get as much info out of him as I could."

"I feel that, but the last time I checked, you ain't the head of this territory yet. Not until the vote."

"So? Gino ain't know that." Boogie and Bentley exchanged a look for a moment before they both started laughing.

"You wild for that. You're lucky I'm a quick nigga. I picked up what you were puttin' down quick!" Bentley said and slapped hands with Boogie. "You ain't have to make my cuz shut down shop though."

"Would you rather he shut down now or when Marco finds out somebody has been stealin' money from him under the table? Especially since he's doin' the shit in what was my pop's territory and will be mine. From the way Caesar is makin' it seem, they don't wanna vote me in. They want someone else at the table. I can't give 'em any reason to think I'm incompetent."

"Well, when we blow these niggas out of the water, then they'll be able to see that we ain't playin'."

"That's the plan."

"You sure you ready for this?" Bentley asked, watching Boogie's face. "I wasn't gon' bring this up, but that night when all that shit went down, you seemed a little shaken up."

"That's 'cause I was," Boogie responded and thought back to that night. He remembered the daze he was in as the bodies dropped around him. "Not in a scary nigga way. But we lost control of the situation, and that ain't never happened to me before."

"That shit happens every day in the hood, but I forgot you grew up in a mansion. Your pops had the same kind of upbringin' as me. Gutter and grime. I know he had it in him to put niggas in their place, but do you? I need to know, if I roll with you, are you gon' do what needs to be done? Your trigger finger can't stall. That can and will cost you your life. Feel me?"

Boogie nodded as Bentley's words played over and over again in his head. Boogie knew he was right. He hadn't realized until then that he'd chosen his path. It wasn't up in the air anymore. The only thoughts that consumed his head since his father's death were replacing him and getting his streets back in order. His streets. That was how he thought of them now. And if he was to be the head of his Family, he would have to not only portray the image but be it as well.

"Like you said, we in this shit together. You already showed me once that you got me, so just know I got you too, G," Boogie told him and started the car. "I'm gon' hit my cousin Tazz up. I'm already knowin' that Shane ain't gon' be up in that apartment without heavy firepower, so we gon' need some too."

"I'm sure Gino would pull up too."

"After what just happened in there?"

"Plug him directly with Marco, and all will be forgiven. Trust me when I say that Gino is the best weapons expert. He does his trade thing, but my cuz can get military-grade weapons, too. Unmarked."

"Ghost guns?" Boogie asked, suddenly impressed.

"Hell yeah."

"Say no more. Marco and my pops did good business together. I'm sure I can set somethin' up. But only if he comes through tomorrow."

"Tomorrow? I thought you were tryin'a body this nigga tonight?"

Boogie looked down the long street toward the apartment complex he now knew that Shane was in. He smirked as he put the car in reverse to leave.

"Nah. I don't wanna be hasty. Let him go to sleep thinkin' he'll get to see his home again."

Chapter 11

Boogie wouldn't consider himself a killer. He was a talented thief. However, he had been pushed. That same night, Boogie dropped Bentley off at his condo. He decided to give him and Roz the place to themselves. He made the choice to go sleep in his old room at his parents' house. Not only did he figure his mother could use the company, but he had to grab a few things.

It was dark as his car approached the family gate, and he knew with the bright lights that the men standing guard didn't recognize him at first. He could see their angry faces soften when they finally figured out who it was when he got closer and rolled his window down. He didn't even have to come to a stop before they pressed the button to let him through.

Out of recent habit, Boogie checked his surroundings when he parked and then got out. He used the house key on his key ring to unlock the door and enter the house. The first thing he noticed was that the alarm didn't go off upon his entry, which was strange. It was a little past ten o'clock, and he was sure his mother didn't have plans to go anywhere. He shut the door behind him and made his way through the dimly lit house to his bedroom.

It had been a while since he'd slept in it, and he wanted to make sure the things he'd stored there were still there. Barry and Dina weren't the kind of parents who snooped through his things, but he could never be too careful. When he reached his room, he looked down toward his parents' room and saw the light from the television danc-ing on the hallway wall. He gave a small smile, knowing his mother had always liked to fall asleep watching her shows.

He flipped the light switch on when he stepped inside of his room, and he got undressed. He kicked his shoes off first and then took off his hoodie and sweatpants so that all that was left on were a wife beater and a pair of briefs. Going to his tall chest of drawers, he pulled out a pair of Ralph Lauren pajama shorts and put them on.

When he was comfortable, Boogie went inside of his grand walk-in closet. It was big enough to fit another bedroom inside, which was why it was the perfect hiding place when he needed it to be. He walked past his wall of shoes and the designer clothes he'd bought and never worn, and he stopped when he got to the back of the closet. Reaching up on the high shelf, he rummaged around until his hands found the box they were looking for. Pulling it down, he noticed the dust on the top and blew it off. The box had some weight to it, which he had expected since he knew what was inside of it. He exited the closet to go sit on his bed. Placing the box next to him, Boogie lifted the top. The first thing he saw was a tactical vest his father had gotten him, and he thought about the words that had come along with it: *"Boy, you ain't bulletproof."*

And he had been right. Boogie's eyes fell on the bullet hole in the chest of the vest, and he reflected on how he'd gotten it when he was 20 years old. It had been a risky job, one where he had to admit that he'd made a mistake. He'd gotten the weekends mixed up when the owner of a luxury home would be out of town. The owner was a businessman, one who Boogie never would have thought would pack a gun. But he was proven wrong when that Smith & Wesson was pointed at his heart. Lucky for him, he had been wearing the vest and was able to make it out with his life. When he went away for college and he and his dad fell out, he'd put it away in his closet.

He set the vest to the side and next wrapped his hand around the butt of a 9 mm pistol. It was the first gun he'd ever purchased with his own money. He'd gotten it from some joker off the street when he was a teenager, and the bodies he'd caught with it only added to the ones already on the gun. He placed it next to the vest and pulled out the last thing in the box: a switchblade.

He flipped it open and tested the blade. He'd stolen it from his father's office when he was in the sixth grade, and he had used it twice since. The first time was on Peter Danksi, a student who attended the same private school as Boogie. Boogie hated that school, mainly because he was one of the only black kids who attended it, but Barry insisted that he go. Both he and Dina felt it was the safest place for him. What they didn't know was that bad seeds were everywhere, and Peter was one of them. One day after school, he and some of the other boys cornered Boogie when he was walking home, and they tried to jump him. What they weren't expecting was for Boogie to pull out the sharp knife and not be afraid to use it. Peter would always have a scar on his face to remind him of the greatest mistake of his life.

"That knife gave me and your daddy hell."

The sound of his mother's voice caught Boogie off guard. He looked up from the knife in his hands and saw her standing in his doorway in her robe and bonnet. She smiled at him, but it wavered when she saw the vest and the gun beside him.

"Mama, what are you doin' awake? I thought you were asleep."

"I thought I heard a noise coming from this bedroom, and I came to see what it was. I should have known it was you," she said and went to sit next to him on the bed. "Of course I thought it was to check on me, but now I see there was another reason you came. What's all this?"

"My box of firsts," Boogie said and flipped the blade closed. He went to put it back inside of the box, but she took it from him and stared at it.

She gave a tiny laugh and shook her head. After a few more seconds she looked back up at him. "I remember when that boy's daddy called Barry. He said that you attacked his son and all those other boys with this knife. Do you remember what you told your daddy when he asked you about it?"

"Yeah," Boogie said and smiled slightly. "I told him that's what they get for tryin'a corner a lion. And then he whooped my ass for not tellin' him what happened."

"As he should have. You almost had the police knocking at our door, and you should feel blessed that they didn't."

"What did he do to make sure they didn't?" Boogie asked curiously.

"You don't need to know," she said with a wink. "But what I will tell you was that after he whooped your butt and sent you to bed, he came and told me how proud he was of his son for standing his ground. That was the day he decided that he would train you. He saw greatness in you, even back then. He wanted you to be better than him."

"Sometimes I feel like he wanted me to be him."

"Sometimes I did too," Dina said and sighed. She cupped Boogie's chin and turned his head to face her and stared deeply into his eyes. "But now he's gone, and you can be your own man. You can leave behind all of what he wanted you to be."

"Nah." Boogie shook his head. "Not until I figure out who did this to him. And even after that, I—"

"What? You're going to take over for him?"

"I'm his only son, Mama. I have to."

"No, you don't. You can go to school and be the chef you wanted to be. Let Julius or somebody run the business like he's been doing."

"But then it won't be our business anymore. Mama, I need to tell you somethin'."

"What, baby?"

"I'm not goin' back to school."

"What the hell do you mean you aren't going back to school? Being a chef is your dream!"

"Is it? Or is cookin' just something I like to do?" Boogie asked himself more than he was asking her. "I already sent the email. I sent it right after he died. It just feels like right now this is more important. My head wouldn't be there. I wouldn't feel right knowin' that everything Pop put in work for went to somebody else. Plus, the vote happens soon, and Caesar says—"

"Caesar," Dina scoffed. "Do you even know the man you're running around with, Boogie?"

"What is that supposed to mean?" Boogie didn't like the tone of her voice.

"It means that you don't know Caesar the way I do, the way Barry did."

"He's helpin' tryin'a find out who killed Pop."

"You sure about that? Caesar might have been the one who did it."

"Why would you say somethin' like that?"

"I'm just saying don't go putting all your trust in Caesar. I mean, has he even told you about his and Barry's history?" She looked at her son's face and saw nothing but more questions there. She shook her head and sighed. "I didn't think so. Caesar and Barry used to be tight. They grew up together from when they were boys. If you saw one, you saw the other. In fact, their close friendship was one of the things that put an end to the Families' feuding. They weren't just best friends. They were like brothers. Did Caesar tell you that he was the best man in our wedding?"

"Nah." Boogie shook his head.

"Did he tell you that he's your godfather?"

Her words hit Boogie's ears, but he wasn't sure if he'd heard her correctly. *Godfather?* Boogie could count on one hand how many times he'd seen Caesar growing up. And he couldn't remember any of those times seeing Barry and Caesar act close like brothers.

"What . . . what happened? Between them, I mean?"

"Caesar's power-hungry ass happened. He tried to start a merger with the Italians behind the other Families' backs. It was something that would have left the other Families on the bottom while Caesar and the Italians prospered. There was a vote, and your father sided with the other Families. They said if Caesar went ahead with the merger and allowed the Italians in their territories, all of them would go to war with him. Including your father."

"So, what happened?"

"Caesar dropped it, and business continued as usual. But his relationship with Barry was never the same again," she said.

"And you're tellin' me all this to say what exactly?"

"Just watch the company you keep, baby. Caesar is the type of man who only helps others to help himself. There is always a motive somewhere."

Dina handed Boogie back the switchblade and kissed him on the cheek. She left as Boogie was still processing everything. *"There is always a motive somewhere."* Those words echoed inside his head, and he thought about how Caesar had approached him about taking Barry's seat at the table. Could it be that he wanted Boogie to take his father's place so that he could manipulate him and control that territory, too? Was it possible that Caesar was Barry's killer? If that was true, then Boogie had no choice but to make sure he was voted into the seat.

Realizing that he could do nothing about anything in that moment, Boogie placed the items back in the box and put them on the ground beside his bed. When he lay down, he thought about the events of the next day. He'd already contacted Tazz and let him know about the recent events in his life. After questioning him like the police, Tazz agreed help Boogie rid Brooklyn of his problem. He'd already had an inkling that something wasn't right, especially with the cleaners getting shot up. He put himself in charge of getting a closer look at the complex Shane was hiding in.

"How you gon' get close enough to do that?" Boogie had asked.

"I'ma make some calls, but I think I know the bitch he's stayin' with," Tazz had replied.

Boogie trusted him to do his thing. He just hoped it would work without Shane catching wind of the storm brewing. When he turned his bedroom light off, Boogie felt an anxiousness similar to that of a kid the night before the first day of school. To release it, Boogie let his thoughts go to Roz, her perfectly sculpted face and her smile. He couldn't lay a hand on why keeping her safe was so important to him. He'd just met her. But he promised himself that nothing would happen to her or Amber.

Sleep crept up on Boogie like a spider stalking from the shadows. When he finally opened his eyes again, the sun was coming up. He blinked a couple of times before sitting up and stretching. The time on the digital clock beside the bed read six in the morning, and Boogie knew it was time to get up. He showered in the bedroom's connecting bathroom and got dressed. That day he opted for a pair of black joggers and an Amiri hoodie to match. From his bedroom closet he grabbed a leather backpack. It was one his mother had gotten for him from Louis Vuitton when she'd traveled to France. He'd never worn it before. It had just been in the closet collecting dust. But that day, it was going to see some action.

He placed the vest, the gun, and the knife from his box of firsts inside of it and threw it over his shoulder. When he left the room, he closed the door quietly behind him, careful not to wake his mother. His last stop in the home was to the kitchen. He grabbed a container filled with a few pieces of fried chicken from the fridge and a bottled water. Without bothering to heat up the chicken, he left. Ever since he was a kid, Boogie had loved to eat cold chicken. He was able to appreciate the flavor of the seasonings with no fear of burning his tongue.

On his way out of the house, Boogie reset the alarm system, giving himself thirty seconds to leave without the front door making a noise. Once he was outside, he walked to where his Ferrari was parked but then stopped. He stared at the car for a few seconds before deciding it wasn't what he wanted to roll around in that day. If Shane was able to figure out where his father's businesses were, then he probably knew what kind of car he drove.

Boogie turned his head and stared at the home's large detached garage with a smirk on his face. Gripping the container in his hands, he walked away from his car and toward the garage. When he was there, he slid the door open, switched on the light, and was standing face-to-face with his father's car collection. Barry didn't mind spending a pretty penny on what he drove around in.

Boogie's hand slid across the side of a blue McLaren 720S as he walked past it. His eyes danced on the pearly white Rolls-Royce Phantom, which had been Barry's everyday car. He passed a BMW and the black Jeep his father had gotten to match his wife's, and he stopped when he reached the stealth black Mercedes. The AMG G 63 SUV was the perfect choice for that day. The tinted windows would prevent whoever from seeing who was behind the driver's side, and although it was a luxury vehicle, the black would help it blend in and be just another SUV. He opened the door and pulled down the driver's sun visor. Just like he had hoped, the key dropped down into the seat. He tossed his bag on the passenger side and set the container in the middle console. Before getting in himself, he pulled out his cell phone and gave Bentley a call. The phone rang only once before he answered.

"I thought you would have been here by now," Bentley said.

"I'm on my way now. You ready for today?"

"Been ready. Gino hit me after we left last night and told me that he started seein' heavy activity in and out of the complex Shane stayin' in. I don't know what that nigga Shane is up to, but it can't be good. He also said he's seen Shane go in and out, but no Shamar."

"I doubt he's stayin' at Shane's jumpoff's crib. But it's all good. We gon' draw that nigga out. Did my cousin hit your line last night?"

"Tazz? Yup. He hit me this mornin' too. He got his people up and movin' around already."

"Yeah, he's thorough. Always been loyal to the Family."

"Good. That's what we need."

"I'ma—" Boogie stopped midsentence when something in the corner of the garage caught his eye.

It had a brown cover over it, but judging by the shape of it, it was another vehicle. Curiosity itched away at him, and before he knew it, he was stepping away from the Benz truck and walking to the corner where the covered vehicle was.

"Yo, you good over there?" Bentley asked.

"Yeah," Boogie said. "I'm finna pull up on you. I'll call you when I get there. Cool?"

"Cool."

Boogie disconnected the call and put the phone back inside his jogger pocket. When he got to the vehicle, he placed his palm on top of the cover and felt the hard metal under it. He balled some of the fabric in his hand and yanked it off the car. He was half expecting to see a wrecked car underneath, but it was brand new. He was staring at a freshly customized Lamborghini Urus. It was all white with black trim, black rims, and dark-tinted windows.

"Damn," Boogie said sadly, picking up the slip of paper that was on the hood of the vehicle. It said that the vehicle had been delivered two days after Barry died. His dad had never even gotten a chance to drive it.

Boogie went around to the driver's door and opened it. The smell of the fresh leather hit his nostrils, and he was unable to contain himself. Before he knew it, he was sitting in the front seat and gripping the steering wheel. The sleek interior was black and gray, and all the headrests had the letter B engraved in what looked like diamonds. When Boogie stared more closely, he realized that they were diamonds. His dad had gone all out on the SUV.

Boogie pulled down the visor, expecting the key to the car to be there, but nothing fell down. He placed his foot on the brake and pressed the ignition button to see if the car would start. The roar of the engine coming on let him know that the key fob was somewhere inside the SUV. He looked all over, even under the seats, but came up empty-handed. Finally, his eyes fell on the glove compartment. Normally, there would have been a lock there, but where one should have been was a small square with a smooth surface. Boogie touched it with a finger to see if it was a button, but it didn't go in. Instead a neon line flashed and went from the bottom to the top of the square.

"Scan successful. Welcome, Boogie," a computerized voice said from the speakers of the SUV.

The glove compartment popped open, and sure enough, there was the key fob. That wasn't all though. The fob was sitting on top of a white envelope that was made out to him with his father's handwriting on it. He grabbed the fob and placed it in the cup holder. Then, hesitantly, he grabbed the envelope. When he opened it, he saw a folded letter inside. He took it out, unfolded it, and began reading it, hearing his father's voice with every word.

Boogie,

If you're reading this letter instead of receiving this gift directly from me, that means either you were snooping through my shit, or I'm dead. And if that's the case, then there is only one thing to say. I love you, son. Even through my anger and tough teachings, I have always loved you. I know having me for a father wasn't always easy, but there was always a method to my madness. I know the deal was for you to come home for a few months and put in some work for your old man and then go back to school, but I only agreed to do so just to see that spark in your eyes again. Not even making the most perfect steak put as much joy on your face as cracking the toughest safe or pulling off the perfect heist. I knew when it was time for you to go back, you would make the right decision and stay, so I bought you something new to ride around in. It saddens me that I won't get to see you continue to grow into the fine man I know you'll be, but it fills my heart with joy to know that you'll take my seat at the table and be three times who I was.

I had hoped to train you more on what it means to be the head of the Family, because it's more than just running our trade. It's about keeping the entire city on lock at all times. It gets ugly, son. Boogie, sometimes it gets really ugly. But you have to have the stomach for it. You have to be merciless, and sometimes that iron fist gets heavy, but you have to do what you have to do. My greatest mistake was showing mercy to a person I at one point trusted the most in the world. And now I'm dead.

I'm sure the other four are looking to fill my seat, especially Caesar. If Diane has any say-so, the vote will go in your favor despite anything he has to say. Normally I would say don't trust anyone, but Diane is good people. If you have any questions, she'll have the answers.

Don't just be good, son. Be great. I have left an updated version of my will with my seal on it with Julius. It states that everything goes to you: the businesses, the house, the cars, and everything in my bank account. It's all yours. I love you.

Watch your back out there.

Boogie flipped the letter over, hoping that his eyes could trace over more of his father's writing, but that was it. He bit back the swarm of emotions coming over him and instead tried to focus on the meaning of the letter. Barry had known someone was after him. Why else would he write a goodbye letter? The words on the paper mixed with his mother's words from last night. Could Caesar really have had something to do with Barry's murder? He found it strange that he never mentioned how close he and his father had been, or that he was his godfather. And even his father had said that someone he had once trusted with his life was the one to betray him.

Boogie was lost in a sea of confusion, and he needed to sort it out.

He exited the car and pocketed the key fob and the letter before going back to the Benz SUV. He shot Bentley a quick text telling him that he was going to be a little late. He had a stop to make.

Chapter 12

Boogie knew that he would find Julius at Barry's first automotive business, Big Wheel. It was normally where the two of them would start their mornings. It was also the place where anyone who worked under Barry would come and drop weekly dues off.

Boogie pulled the Benz truck into the parking lot backward. Both garage doors were open, and he could see the crew working on a few luxury cars that morning. Boogie turned the vehicle off, got out, and headed toward the business entrance. The crew shot respectful waves his way when they saw him but stayed focused on what they were doing. When he walked in, he saw Will, the business manager, at the counter wearing his dark blue work dickie. He was a short and stout man with a face full of graying hair. Boogie didn't know his exact age, but he had to be been up there with his father. He'd been in the middle of putting something into the computer system, but when he looked up and saw Boogie, his lips spread into a smile.

"I was wondering when you were going to make your way down here, boy!" he said, coming around the counter. The two men shook hands and had a quick embrace. "Where the hell you been?"

"Just handlin' some business," Boogie stated, opting to keep it short. "Plus, I couldn't bring myself to come here since this was where it happened."

"No doubt," Will said, not pressing the subject. "Well, it's good to see you. This place ain't been the same since Barry left us, and Julius ain't no Barry, I'll tell you that much. But we're doing what we gotta do."

"Speakin' of Julius, is he here?"

"Yup. He's in the back office doing counts. All those knuckleheads done rolled up in here with their money, so I'm sure he's back there doing counts."

"Good lookin'."

Boogie left Will at the counter and went down the hallway that led to the back offices. Although Julius had his own office, for some reason he knew he would find him in Barry's. He pushed the slightly ajar door completely open and entered the office. He saw Julius sitting at the desk with his feet kicked up and a stack of money in his hands.

When he saw Boogie standing there, he flashed his pearly white teeth. "Neph! What's good with you?"

"I don't know. You tell me. I haven't heard much from you lately," Boogie said with a shrug.

"You know shit been crazy in our camp. I'm just tryin'a make sure the ship is still sailing. That's what Barry would have wanted."

"No, he would have wanted you to find whoever did this to him." Boogie couldn't keep the distaste from his tone.

"And don't you think that's what I've been doing?" Julius said with a concerned look on his face.

"No. It looks like you're getting too comfortable in his office. My office."

"It's about my feet on the desk? All right, I'll fix it." Julius sat up and put his feet on the floor. "How's that?"

The two men stared each other down before they both broke into grins. Julius set the money in his hands down and got up to pull Boogie into a tight embrace. When he let him go, he rubbed the side of Boogie's face. "You good?"

"Nah. Still just tryin'a make sense of all this. But I don't think I can."

"You and me both," Julius said, patting Boogie's cheek before going back to the desk. Before he sat down, he paused. "You mind if I sit back down at your desk?"

"Man, stop playin' with me," Boogie said with a smile.

"Shit, I was just checkin'. You rolled up in here like you were on that."

Julius resumed his place behind the wooden desk, and Boogie sat in a cushioned seat across from it.

"My bad, Unc. I been on edge a little bit lately."

"Would it happen to have something to do with the shooting that took place at the cleaners the other day?"

"You know about that, huh?"

"Why wouldn't I? You know information moves through the streets fast. Plus, your mom called and told me everything."

"Did she also tell you that she was in there tryin'a sell it?" Boogie asked and watched a shocked expression come over Julius's face.

"That she didn't say a thing about. She was trying to get rid of the business?"

"Let her tell it, she wants to get rid of all of my pop's businesses."

"Hmm, that's interesting."

"Yeah, especially because now she really can't. My dad left them all to me."

"How do you know that?"

"He left me a letter and said you have the updated will."

"Oh, yeah. You're right." Julius seemed genuinely surprised that Boogie knew about the will, and that made Boogie's brow furrow.

"You did plan on tellin' me about it, right?"

"Of course I did, neph. But just like you, I've been so busy handling business around here that it seems to have slipped my mind. Give me a second. It's in my office. I'll go grab it for you."

He left the room and within a few minutes was back. In his hands was a thick envelope that he handed to Boogie as he passed. Boogie was happy to see that the red seal was still in place. He stared at their family crest before peeling the white envelope open. He removed the documents and skimmed them. As Barry had said, he'd left everything to his son. The accounts, the cars, the mansion, and even their vacation homes in California and their cabin in Denver. The next page detailed all of the businesses Boogie now owned as well as how to run them.

He glanced up at Julius with a befuddled expression. "He left me everything."

"Everything?"

"Everything. When did he do this?"

"A few months ago," Julius told him with an indifferent expression. "I never looked at the documents."

"Do you think he knew he was about to die?"

"Maybe. Old spiritualists say that we can sometimes sense when our time is coming."

"I think he did." Boogie shook the papers. "I think he did this because he knew how the other Families would be toward me. I think he wanted to ensure my place beside them."

"I reckon," Julius said, "even from the grave Barry is still looking out for you. Is there anything else in there?"

Boogie turned the pages all the way to the last one and shook his head. The only name on the will was his. Barry hadn't even left anything to Dina, but Boogie assumed it was because he knew his son would make sure she was taken care of.

"Nah. Nothing else." Boogie folded the papers and put them back inside the envelope. "Thanks, Unc. I gotta head out. You good over here?"

"Just keepin' your seat warm, baby boy."

"A'ight, I'm out."

"Let me walk you to the door," Julius offered.

"Cool."

The two of them walked and made small talk until they reached the front door of the establishment. Boogie gave Will, who was on the phone scheduling a car detail, a nod before extending a hand to Julius.

"We family, boy. Come here." Julius slapped his hand away and gave Boogie another hug. "You be safe out there."

"No doubt."

"I see you're pushing one of your daddy's toys today." Julius took note of the Benz truck in the parking lot. "Tell me, is that the one that's bulletproof?"

"You already know."

"Good. Because you might need it."

"Rather have it and not need it then need it and not have it! A'ight, Unc, I love you. I'ma catch you later."

"Love you too."

With that, Boogie was gone.

Chapter 13

Boogie had Tazz and Gino meet him and Bentley at an old insurance building that Barry had purchased a few months prior. He had plans to turn it into the second location of Big Wheel Automotive. Nobody but Boogie knew about it, so it was a safe meeting spot. The inside of the building had a bunch of wooden boards lying around and debris from the drywall. It looked like whatever construction company had been hired stopped in the middle of the job. No doubt that was because of Barry, but now that Boogie knew he was the new owner of everything that had been his father's, he was going to make sure the job was finished. However, at that moment, leaning on a wall would have to do.

Tazz and Gino arrived minutes apart from each other, both dressed similarly to Boogie and Bentley.

"Man, all this dust and shit is fuckin' up the Yeezys!" Tazz complained, looking around at the mess.

"What you gon' be sayin later when you got blood on 'em?" Bentley asked, shaking his head.

"Pssh, nigga, I don't know about you, but I ain't never get blood on my shoes," Tazz told him. "The voice on the phone belonged to you, so you must be Bentley. So, who is he?" He pointed to where Gino was sitting with his elbows resting on his knees.

"That's my cousin Gino I was tellin' you about. The one who told us where Shane was hidin' at."

"Aw, you mean the nigga who couldn't get eyes on the inside," Tazz said, and Gino smacked his teeth.

"Ain't nobody ask me all that," he corrected him. "They asked where Shane was at, and I came through with the info."

"I'm just fuckin' with you. Chill out, man. We all had a part to play in this," Tazz said and turned to Boogie. He reached in a pocket of his pants and pulled out a piece of paper. "Ol' girl ya boy is stayin' with."

"Stephanie?" Gino asked curiously.

"Yeah. She works at the club Diane runs. I used to see her from time to time when I, uh, stopped by there."

"Stopped by, huh?" Boogie said sarcastically.

"Look, my dealings there ain't nobody's business but mine."

"It seems like everybody knows Stephanie. We sure we can trust her? Especially if she got wrapped up in a nigga like Shane?"

"She owes me. I stopped a nigga from almost killin' her one night, and I cashed in on that favor."

"What you mean?"

"Look and see for yourself," Tazz said and handed him the paper in his hand.

Boogie unfolded it to see exactly what Tazz was talking about. It was a drawing, but not just any drawing. It was a blueprint of Stephanie's floor. It showed that she lived on the second floor and the setup of that very floor. She'd drawn a hallway with the other apartments that led to hers at the end of the hall. She'd even drawn the inside of her home with the fire escape connected to her bedroom window.

"Look on the back," Tazz instructed.

"Damn," Boogie said when he did. There Stephanie had written down everything Shane had to do and rough time frames. "Good lookin'."

"No doubt," Tazz told him. "I met her at the job as soon as we got off the phone last night. Apparently she ain't too happy with the way he's been treatin' her lately."

"Well, it seems like a woman scorned is my best friend," Boogie said, passing the paper to Bentley and Gino.

"Yo, Boog, did you see this?" Bentley asked after looking over the paper. "It says here that Shane is takin' his truck to get fixed today at four o'clock."

"Yeah, I saw it."

"Did you see where?"

Boogie took the piece of paper back from him and looked to where Bentley was talking about. He could barely make out Stephanie's handwriting, but he tried. "Yeah, it says he's takin' the truck to BW's," Boogie said, and it clicked as soon as it was out of his mouth. His eyes grew wide, and he looked back up at Bentley. "He's takin' a hit on Big Wheel."

"Not if we can stop it," Tazz cut in. "We know when this nigga is planning on doin' it. We just gotta get to him before then."

"How the fuck we gon' do that? That nigga keeps an army around him at all times. We ain't gon' be able to get through them without getting killed or injured badly," Gino stated, and Boogie had to agree.

"Who's sayin' anything about goin' through his soldiers?" Bentley asked. He turned to Boogie. "I was thinkin' more of a 'get in and get out without bein' seen' type plan."

"I'm listenin'," Boogie told him.

"Have you ever seen the movie *Colombiana?*"

The sound of glass shattering caught the attention of three men who were standing in the back of the Brick Heights apartment complex. Jumping into action, they all looked to see where the noise had come from and saw a man in tattered clothing staggering toward them. He was mumbling something in drunken slurs that none of them could understand. He continued to get closer to them, and they clutched their poles.

"Ay, motherfucka, you need to get the fuck on somewhere," one of them warned with his hand around the handle of the gun in his pants. "Yo, did you hear what the fuck I just said?"

"D, he's a drunk. Chill out. He probably can't even tell you where he's at right now."

"I don't give a fuck," D said, pulling out his gun and approaching the man who was having a hard time walking in a straight line. "Eric, watch my back since this nigga Bone is bein' a bitch."

D, a young man in his mid-twenties, grabbed the drunk by his arm and pulled back the thin hood he was wearing. Minus the wear and tear, and the fact that it was obvious life was kicking the man's ass, he didn't look to be too much older than D. He had a scar that had long since healed on his cheek, and his eyes were bloodshot. He smelled so badly of alcohol and cigarettes that D turned his nose up.

"You a smelly-ass nigga, you know that?" D asked and nudged the man's head with his gun.

"Drank . . . I dropped my drank," the man slurred, trying to focus on D's face. "Give me a few dollars to get another. Y'all owe me."

"You think money grows on trees?" D scoffed. "Shit, maybe you do. That's why you're walkin' around stinkin' and shit. If you want some money outta me, you gon' have to dance like a monkey or somethin'."

"I ain't dancing like no monkey to impress a monkey!" the man exclaimed. "Your mama musta fucked a gorilla to make something as ugly as you!"

Eric and Bone snickered behind D, and he glared at them. He didn't think anything was funny, especially the thought of getting played by a homeless man. He shoved him hard, making him fall to the ground.

"Get the fuck on before shit has to get ugly," D warned.

"I ain't leavin' here until you tell that motherfucka Shane I said I want my money!"

His words caught D off guard as he got back to his feet. Behind him, Eric and Bone exchanged looks. Silently they were asking each other the same question, and that question was, how did a drunk man know where Shane was lying low?

"Ain't nobody by the name Shane here," D growled.

"Lyin'-ass nigga! He's here and I want my money. I did a job for him while he was here weeks ago. He said he was gon' give me five hundred dollars. I done gone through all my Hen . . . Hennessy bottles waitin', and I can't wait no more. I want my money!"

His voice was getting too loud, and D felt he had no other choice but to hit him in the jaw. The man fell to the ground again easily, but when he got back up, he went back to shouting about the money Shane supposedly owed him. He was relentless. D wanted to shoot him right then and there, but he didn't want to blow up Shane's spot. He would be a dead man walking if he did that. Plus, it was too early in the day, and there was a lot of traffic in and out of the complex. Normally people didn't come to the back, but still, nobody would be able to ignore a gunshot or a dead body on the concrete. D groaned as he looked at the man and figured it would be best to take him to see Shane and let him sort it out.

"A'ight, man. What's your name?" D asked.

"Alfonzo," he answered.

"And you say Shane owes you money? A'ight. Let's go see about that." D grabbed him by the arm and forced him to walk. "And I hope you're right about it. Because Shane doesn't take too lightly to people wastin' his time."

"And I don't take too lightly to people not payin' me what they owe!" Alfonzo snatched away. "I might be drunk, but I can walk my damn self. I might sidestep a bit, but I'll get there! Now hurry up so I can get my money, or else everybody is gon' know that this outsider is in Brooklyn."

Bone and Eric chuckled, and D shot them irritated looks. He still didn't find dude funny. The only thing Alfonzo had was a lot of nerve.

"Bone, you come with me," he said, "just in case this nigga tries some funny shit when we get inside."

Bone nodded and opened the door they had all been standing in front of. Once they were inside, D pushed Alfonzo toward a carpeted staircase. Alfonzo stumbled up the steps on the way to the second floor, but like he had told D, he got there.

"D, I don't think Shane owes him any money, man," Bone said in a low tone.

"I don't think he does either, but it's either blow his head off outside or somewhere we can easily clean it up," D said with a shrug.

They walked to the end of the hallway on the second floor until they got to apartment 201. D knocked twice before the door swung open, and he was met by a man holding a semi-automatic. He nodded his greeting at D and Bone, but when his eyes fell on the man in ragged clothes with them, he turned his lip up.

"Who is the smelly nigga?"

"Somebody who knows Shane is here," D said to him. "He claims he owes him some money. And if he doesn't get his money, he's willin' to sing to the world that we're in Brooklyn."

"Why you ain't just handle that downstairs?"

"'Cause, nigga, that would be stupid. Too many eyes and ears."

"A'ight, man," the man at the door said with a sigh. "But that's your ass. You know Shane don't like random popups after what happened the last time he was here. He in the back."

He stepped aside and let them in. There were five other men inside the apartment. Some were counting money, and others were smoking. Alfonzo began looking all around the apartment, and D didn't like that. He shoved him hard.

"Ay, keep your eyes straight, motherfucka," he instructed.

When they reached the back den, D knocked on one of the double doors and waited for it to open. He noticed that Bone was standing a little ways away from them. Before he could turn to acknowledge it, one of the doors opened. Shane stood there staring at him with annoyance in his eyes that quickly turned into fire when he saw Alfonzo standing there.

"Who the fuck is this?"

"He said you owe him some money, boss," D told him.

"Nigga, are you stupid? I don't owe nobody in this city no fuckin' money. Please don't tell me that's the reason your dumb ass brought him up here. I'ma kill you, you know that, right?"

"He . . . he knew where to find you already though, boss," Bone spoke up from behind them. "He walked right up to us and started talkin' too loud."

"Yeah, that's why we brought him up here. I couldn't handle him the way I wanted to while we were down-stairs. Name's Alfonzo."

Shane—whose face was still healing, but he refused to wear a bandage any longer—eyed all of them before resting his gaze on Alfonzo. He studied him almost as if he were trying to recognize him. He clenched both of his hands into fists before slowly unclenching, and he let out a loud, bearlike shout.

"You two, get the fuck out of here," Shane said to D and Bone. "When I'm done with this motherfucka, you're gon' have an idea of what I'll do to you if you ever do some shit like this again."

D and Bone only needed to be told once. When they were gone, Shane motioned for Alfonzo to enter the bedroom and told the other men to get out. "And don't come back in here until I tell you to, understand?"

"Got it, boss," the three men said in unison as they exited.

When Shane and Alfonzo were alone, Shane closed the door and locked it. It was obvious that the bedroom was a lady's bedroom, with the pink comforter set and the silver decor along the walls. Alfonzo's eyes brushed the walls before he turned to Shane and glared at him.

"You don't scare me, you slimy motherfucka. I want my money!" Alfonzo slurred.

Shane stared at him in disgust. "You really came all the way over here to risk your life for ten dollars?" he asked.

"Five hundred!"

"Same difference," Shane said and looked curiously at him. "I've heard of liquid courage, but I ain't never heard of liquid suicide. Who sent you?"

"What the hell you talkin' about? I sent me, mother-fucka!" Alfonzo said, taking a step toward Shane.

With one swift punch, Shane knocked him back into one of the chairs against the wall. Alfonzo's hand flew to his cheek, and he hunched over.

"I can tell when somebody is lyin' to me." Shane turned his nose up. "You one of Boogie's people?"

"You know what your first mistake was?" Alfonzo said with a chuckle.

"What?"

"You didn't make sure I wasn't strapped."

Faster than Shane could blink, Alfonzo pulled a gun from his ankle. He pointed it directly at Shane's forehead. Shane also noticed that the slurred speech was gone and there was a fire in his eyes. In the distance outside of the apartment, Shane could hear gunfire, and he was confused. What was happening? The door to the room bust open, and Alfonzo switched his aim to the three men running into the room. He fired his gun three times and dropped them all before they could even really see what was happening. The front door of the apartment was kicked in, and from the back room they could see glimpses of all of Shane's men being gunned down.

"What the fuck?" Shane's eyes grew big, and he turned back to Alfonzo. "Who the hell are you, Alfonzo?"

"First, my name ain't really Alfonzo. It's Tazz. Second, you asked me earlier who I work for. Well, I work for him." He motioned the gun in his hand to something behind Shane.

The ruckus in the house had been so loud that he hadn't even heard the window that led to the fire escape open. When he turned around, he was face-to-face with Boogie. He tried to grab for the gun on his waist, but Tazz cocked his gun.

"Try it and I'ma wet your shirt up." He snatched the gun from Shane's waist and the one on his ankle.

"Good work, Tazz," Boogie said to the man who had been introduced to Shane as Alfonzo.

"No problem, cuz. Handle your business," Tazz said.

Boogie pulled out his own pistol and pointed it at Shane, who glared back at him. He was angry at himself for once again being on the wrong end of the gun.

"You should really treat the women in your life better," Boogie taunted. "Because shit like this can happen. All your shooters' blood is in the streets, and it's on your hands."

It clicked with Shane that he had been set up, and his own people had accidently served him on a platter to his enemies. It was funny actually, so funny that he had to laugh. What started as a low chuckle turned into an all-out bellow.

"So you found me. Good for you." He feigned clapping his hands.

"Yup, and before you could make a hit on Big Wheel."

"Make a hit on Big Wheel? Now why would I do that?"

"We know you're plannin' on goin' there today."

"Okay. That don't mean I'm goin' to shoot it up." Shane chuckled again. "The only reason I shot up the cleaners was because I knew you were there."

"Then why go?"

Shane stared into Boogie's face. He could tell there were many thoughts crossing his mind right then, and most of them probably didn't make sense to him. He wanted to laugh because he really had no clue what was going on around him. Boogie was so naive, too naive, and truthfully Shane had zero pity for him. The thought of everything that had taken place in the background caused a deep, crazed laugh to seep through his lips.

"What you findin' so funny? 'Cause ain't nobody else in here laughing. I asked you a question, so answer."

"I'll pass. I have a question for you though. Don't you want to know how your father died?"

It was so random, and Shane could tell that it had thrown Boogie off. Shane's eyes went to the gun in Boogie's hand and waited for it to lower. Boogie's hand wavered slightly, but the pistol stayed pointed at Shane.

"Yo, what the fuck did you just say?" Boogie asked.

"You heard me, nigga," Shane said with a slow smile forming on his mouth. "Do you want to know how he died? Because I can tell you. They did unthinkable things to that man, and he screamed like a girl the entire time. And when they got to choppin' off his toes, well, if the streets had heard him, they would have called your dad a whole ho."

The last words out of Shane's mouth were his trigger. Boogie smacked Shane across the face with his gun. The force was so powerful that Shane saw one of his own teeth hit the floor. Shane groaned in pain because Boogie had hit the side that had been shot.

"Boog," Tazz said from the corner. "He's just tryin'a rile you up. Hold your head."

"Yeah," Shane panted and spat out a glob of blood. "Listen to your mans, Boog."

"Stop speakin' on shit you don't know about then."

"You just can't be as dumb as you look. Do you think I made that shit up? The details about his death weren't in the media. Ask yourself how I know."

"Because you did it."

"Mmm, no. I wish I could take the credit for that, but I can't. But do you think me bein' in New York at the same time your old man was gunned down was a coincidence? Do you really think there is no connection at all? Think about it. How could we have made that much money under the radar in your city without anyone knowing about it? How could we have moved so freely? It was all part of the plan, and getting Barry out of the way was only a small part of it. Pretty soon, you'll all be out of the way."

"Boog, off this nigga now. We're too hot out here. One of the neighbors probably already called the police. Bentley and Gino are probably outside right now waitin' for us."

"He knows somethin'," Boogie said to Tazz and then turned back to Shane. "Tell me who killed him."

"Fuck you," Shane said and spat on his feet.

"Then I'm gon' make your daddy mourn you the same way I'm mourning my dad."

Before he could finish his sentence, Shane quickly reached and grabbed the hand that Boogie was holding the gun with. Boogie pulled the trigger, but Shane had already moved out of the way and made him drop the gun. He had a grip on Boogie's wrist and grabbed his elbow to turn him around so that he blocked Tazz's aim.

"You know who killed your dad just like I know who did. Those close brotherhoods never seem to last, do they?"

Shane said. "And it's not over yet. Soon, y'all gon' just be a memory. It's time for new blood. We're gon' take ov—"

Those were the last words Shane spoke before Boogie broke the grip he had on him. Shane had been expecting Boogie to go for his gun. He never expected a bare fist to meet his face. Boogie began plowing into him with combination punches so fast that Shane couldn't block any of them. Each blow felt like he was being hit with a weight, and he was never able to catch his breath. His head bounced back from each punch until he was on his back again, and even then, the hits didn't stop. His head bounced off the ground, and he felt the life draining out of him. That time, he knew he wasn't going to be able to come back from the dead. He felt the wetness from his own blood underneath the back of his head and knew it was over for him. Soon, he didn't even feel Boogie's punches. In fact, he didn't feel anything. The only thing he saw was Boogie finally pick his gun up from the floor and aim it at his face.

"Let's do it right this time," he said, and Shane closed his eyes before the final shots rang out.

Boom! Boom! Boom!

Chapter 14

The sound of many feet marching with a purpose bounced off the concrete walls of a tunnel beneath an old butcher's shop. There was a flame in the pit of Shamar Hafford's stomach that grew by the second. He'd just received news that his son, his only child, had been killed right before he arrived in New York. He'd sent Julius and Shane ahead of him so that he could wrap up some business in Ohio. His son's death just went to show that right up to Shane's final moments on the earth, he couldn't do anything right. He was supposed to be lying low somewhere off the radar, not at some whore's house. He'd almost ruined everything for Shamar, but thankfully he hadn't. Shamar's business associates normally came to him. That time he felt that it was time for it to be the other way around.

When they reached the end of the tunnel, they could go either left or right. He'd been directed to go right by his associate, so he did. At the end of that hall, there was a tall metal door, and a man was standing outside of it. He had almond skin, and like Shamar, he wore a suit. When he saw the group of men approaching him, he nodded his head and opened the door.

"He is expecting you," he said with a heavy accent.

"I know," Shamar said and adjusted his cuff links.

He walked into a fully furnished room that had red carpet, a pool table, and a stage with a pole. Shamar didn't give a second glance to the topless women dancing around it to the music playing. Nor did he care that everyone's eyes in the room had turned to him and his entourage. His attention was on a man sitting at the bar wearing a taupe suit. Shamar motioned to his men to let them know they'd come as far as they could. He approached the bar alone, and the man sitting there saw him and stood up.

He stood at average height and wore a hat over his gray hair. Over his top lip was a thick mustache, and he had a few wrinkles over his face. The dark energy around him matched Shamar's, and that made them the perfect business partners.

"Bosco," Shamar greeted the Italian with a handshake.

"Shamar, my friend!" Bosco said with a thick accent. "I would ask how you are doing, but I heard about the loss of your son in Brooklyn yesterday. Sorry for your loss."

"Not as sorry as I am," Shamar responded in a bored tone. He gestured toward two barstools. "Shall we?"

"Of course," Bosco said, and the two of them sat down facing each other. "Dia, come over here."

Bosco motioned for the very sexy chocolate-skinned bartender to make her way to them. Shamar wasn't one to stare too long at any woman, but she was something special. She wore her natural hair cut low, and she had the juiciest lips he'd ever seen in his life. Her body was slim and her breasts were small, but her hips were wide, and she had a plump—

"What can I get for you and your very handsome friend, sir?"

Her sweet voice interrupted Shamar's unsavory thoughts. She batted the long eyelashes on her slanted eyes at him and smiled.

"How about you pour us two shots from that new 1942 bottle, my dear," Bosco told her.

"Your wish is my command," she said.

It didn't take her long to pour their shots. And when she brought them back, she was sure to let her hand brush against Shamar's when she gave him his. He lifted the shot to her before tossing it back and placing the glass back on the bar. The shot was strong, but Shamar welcomed the sensation that came with it trickling down his throat.

"That's some good shit," Bosco stated, sucking his teeth. He placed his empty glass down next to Shamar's and turned his attention back to him. "Minus this little setback, is everything else going as planned?"

"So far everything has played out exactly how you said, except for my son's indiscretions, but fortunately for us that problem is gone now. I loved my son, but saying that I liked him would be a stretch. He was incompetent and had too much of his worthless mother in him. The only good thing that came out of Shane's work was Barry Tolliver's death. That being said, Julius has been quite helpful."

"Yes. I spoke with him earlier today. He tells me that Caesar is so focused on who killed Barry that he hasn't even noticed his empire crumbling underneath him. He's going to wish he'd done that business deal all those years ago. They all will. They denied me, so I'm going to break them down from the inside."

"They're fools to think their Pact could hold up for years," Shamar added. "Peace never lasts."

"It doesn't, but I hope ours does."

Bosco was speaking of the deal he and Shamar had made. The two had met years prior when Bosco was looking for a new connect. After meeting Shamar one time, he had to have Shamar's product in Staten Island. When Bosco presented him with an opportunity to expand over all of New York, he jumped at the opportunity. So what if they had to knock people out of the way? It would all be worth it in the end. Once the Five Families had fallen, the two of them had agreed that Bosco would take over and Shamar would continue to be his connect to the finest cocaine Ohio had to offer. It was just the kind of business Shamar needed. The only thing was that Bosco had needed Shamar to do all of the muscle work. The Families had been keeping a watchful eye on him for years. It would have been hard for him to move how he wanted to alone.

"As long as we both hold up our end of the bargain, I don't see any problem with our deal," Shamar said.

"Good," Bosco said, clapping his hands and wearing a big smile. "Now the only thing left to do is to get rid of Caesar. He is the strongest link of them all. Without him, the others will fold."

"I agree. What do you have in mind?"

"I have something in the works. You'll know soon enough. In the meantime, I have a gift for you."

"A gift?" Shamar asked, raising a curious brow.

"Yes, for all of your hard work," Bosco said and held his hand up.

Dia saw it and came back over to them. Bosco took her hand in his and kissed it before holding it out to Shamar. He hesitated, but after a beat Shamar took it. There was something about her dazzling gaze that was enchanting.

"Take him into the back room and show him our gratitude," Bosco told her, and she nodded.

"Follow me," she said to Shamar in a sexy tone.

Shamar smoothed his tie and got up from the barstool. Bosco grinned at him and nodded his approval, even though he didn't need it. Dia led Shamar away from Bosco and through a doorway that was covered by thick, beaded curtains. There was a hallway with doors on either side, but she led him to the last door on the right. Inside, there was a comfortable leather couch, a mini fridge, and a large flat-screen television hanging on the wall.

"Sit down," Dia said and pushed him on the couch.

She gave him a better look at her formfitting black mesh dress when she stood in front of him. Shamar unbuttoned the jacket of his suit and slid it off so that he could be more comfortable. She grinned at him and sat on his lap.

"You must be a very powerful man if Bosco respects you, Shamar."

"I'm just a man who likes doing good business," he told her simply.

He didn't know if it was her accent or the way his name rolled off her tongue that made the tip of his dick tingle. Ever since his divorce, one of Shamar's favorite pastimes was indulging in the art of women half his age. He was already a powerful man, but being desired by younger women did a thing for his already-oversized ego. His hand made its way down the small of her back and onto her plump butt. It was softer than he imagined it would be.

"You like to get straight to it, don't you?" she asked with a grin.

"I didn't come back here for my health," Shamar said and pushed her off his lap.

She didn't complain. Instead, she got on her knees, unzipped his pants, and pulled them, along with his briefs, down to his thighs. He placed the gun that had been on his hip on the arm of the chair, far enough away from her but close enough to grab it himself if he needed to. His one-eyed monster was standing at attention and looking her square in the face. With no shame, she put her lips around the head and moved her wet mouth down his shaft. Soon the sucking and slurping sounds of her pleasuring him filled the room. Watching a pretty thing like herself in such a submissive position turned him on to a point of no return. When she switched from just sucking to adding the two-handed twist combo with it, Shamar let his head fall back onto the back of the couch. His eyes were lowered in pleasure, and he was okay with letting her suck the nut out of him, but she was hungry for more.

"I need to feel this big dick inside of me right now," she said, removing him from her mouth.

She pulled a condom from her bust and gave it to him to put on when she stood up and removed her dress. She was completely naked underneath, and her dark brown nipples made his mouth water. As soon as he rolled the condom down his manhood, Dia climbed on top and straddled him. She positioned him at her wet opening and slid down. As his dick fought against her tightness, he reached behind her and slapped and squeezed her ass cheeks.

"Mmm," she moaned when he was all the way inside. "Just lie back and relax. Let me do all the work, baby."

And that she did. Dia took him on a ride he would never forget. She bounced up and down on him like her knees would never give out. Shamar's breathing was rigid because even with the condom on he couldn't deny how good her pussy felt around his thick meat. Dia placed her breasts in front of his face while she rode him, and Shamar sucked and nibbled on her nipples while she went for her orgasm.

"Ohh! I'm cumming," she moaned and began to ride him harder.

He too felt an electrical current shooting straight to his tip. He held on to let go himself until he felt her shoot her juices. He held her hips tightly and thrust up deeply into her as he felt the release of his own orgasm. He held back his moan by biting his lip, and when the feeling subsided, he caught his breath. She rubbed the side of his face tenderly before climbing off his now-limp penis. Shamar removed the condom and tossed it into a wastebasket that was underneath where the television was hanging. Dia put her dress back on, and Shamar pulled his pants back up.

"Maybe I'll see you again," she said in a hopeful tone.

"You've served your purpose," he told her flatly.

Just because he liked sex with younger women didn't mean he wanted more than that from them. They were a distraction and needy. There was only one thing he was willing to give them, and that was sex. Anything else they could get from another.

Shocked at his response, Dia shot him a dirty look and stormed out of the room. Shamar didn't understand why women got upset when a person told them the truth. A common misunderstanding between men and women was that sex brought forth a deeper connection. The truth was, if the connection wasn't already in existence before the act, most likely there wouldn't be one.

He put his suit jacket back on and left the room. When he emerged from the back room, he saw that Dia had taken a seat on Bosco's lap. She glared at him before looking away. Shamar gave Bosco a nod farewell before departing with his people.

Chapter 15

Some time had passed and Boogie had finally handled Shane. Even though that problem was out of the way, the bigger issue was Shamar. Boogie kept his pole on him at all times just in case there was some sort of retaliation behind it. But so far, the streets had been quiet. Not only that, but it was finally time for the vote to take place. Boogie hadn't seen too much of Caesar, but he was okay with that, especially with the things that were on his mind. Shane's last words ran over and over in Boogie's head. He couldn't seem to escape them no matter how hard he tried.

"Those close brotherhoods never seem to last, do they?"

There was something about the way Shane had said it. The only brotherhoods Barry had were with Julius and Caesar. And although Boogie could admit that Julius had been acting strange lately, he chalked it up to being under so much pressure. Boogie couldn't see him crossing his father any more than he could have seen himself doing so. So that left Caesar.

It hadn't made sense to Boogie that Caesar King, *the* Caesar King, still didn't have the slightest clue who was behind it or why. The only reason Boogie could think of for that was if he was the one behind it. It had been in his face the whole time, and he couldn't believe he had missed it. He was angry at himself for being around him all that time and not seeing it until then. He felt like a fool. Caesar probably was getting a real laugh out of it.

Boogie vowed to hold his peace until after the vote that day. And when he pulled up to the high-rise building the meeting was going to be at, he composed himself. Even though his gut feeling was enough to go on, he wouldn't seek revenge on Caesar until he had some solid proof. When he stepped out of the Lamborghini, the breeze nipped at his ears. The fall had snuck up on him. In another time he would have been sitting in culinary class preparing to make a dish he never had before. Now he was on his way to find out if he would be deemed worthy to run his Family's business. He'd come dressed for the occasion, wearing Tom Ford from top to bottom. The black turtleneck protected his neck from the windchill, and the gold chains around his neck gleamed in the sunlight. He checked the time on the Patek on his wrist and handed his keys to the valet.

"Get a scratch on my whip and you'll regret it for the rest of your life," Boogie warned the young kid, whose eyes grew wide.

"You have nothing to worry about, sir," he stammered.

"Good."

Boogie left him to park his car and followed the instructions he'd been given to get to the meeting room. He took the elevator, and when the double doors shut, he pressed the number fifteen. When the elevator didn't budge, he remembered the key card in his pocket. He pulled it out and held it over the card reader by the floor numbers. It turned green, and the elevator began going up. It didn't take long to get to his destination, and when the elevator doors opened, there were two men in suits there waiting to escort him.

They brought him to a big room that had a beautiful view of Manhattan, and they closed the door behind him. In the middle of the room, there was a big, round wooden table with five cushioned chairs around it. It was funny, really. The room looked exactly how he imagined. He noticed Caesar staring at him when he walked in, but he didn't budge or say a word. Marco and Li nodded at him when he entered, but Diana stood up and embraced him.

"Boogie, my dear boy," she said and gripped his hands in hers when she broke the embrace.

"Hi, Diana," Boogie said.

He was no stranger to her. In fact, she used to babysit him sometimes when he was little. He remembered that causing some huge fights between his parents. Dina swore up and down that Barry was having an affair with her. But as Boogie grew older, he realized that the two were just close friends. However, what Barry did when he was inside of her club was a different story. He knew his father wasn't a faithful man, but Barry came home every night, and he took care of his family.

"I'm sorry I wasn't able to stay long for the funeral or come to the repast," she told him. "I had to say goodbye to my old friend in my own way. Staring at that closed casket just made me think about the horror under it, and I just didn't want to remember Barry that way."

"I understand," Boogie said and kissed her knuckles. "He would have understood too. He loved you."

"And I him," she said, smiling fondly at Boogie.

"All right, let's get down to business," Caesar said, interrupting their rapport. "Boogie, come stand next to Barry's seat please."

Boogie stared at him for a moment. He fought back the rush of emotions coming to him all at once. He didn't like how he spoke Barry's name so freely. Caesar's forehead wrinkled slightly at the glare he was getting.

"Boogie, did you hear him?" Diana asked.

"Yeah, I did," Boogie said.

He went and stood beside his father's chair. All eyes were on him, but he kept his on Caesar. He was imagining the different ways he would kill him. So far, shooting him off a tall building was his favorite.

"Let's begin," Li said, clasping his hands together and causing Boogie to finally break his gaze. "Caesar told us about how you handled a recent situation in Brooklyn quickly before it got out of control."

"But there was a huge cleanup," Marco spoke up. "There were more than ten bodies. Do you know how much it cost to pay off the Families, let alone make sure it didn't hit the news?"

"Marco, one word: Harlem," Diana said, cutting her eyes at him as he leaned back into his seat.

"That was years ago. Plus, it was a different time back then," he grumbled.

"I personally don't see a difference. And I believe we had to clean up twenty bodies with your trigger-happy ass," she told him and averted her attention back to Boogie. "You exhibited great leadership skills."

"But the question at hand is, can you run an entire operation?" Li asked. "The responsibility is higher, and the risks are greater. How do we know that we can trust you?"

"With all due respect, I'ma just put it to you all like this and let you do with it what you're gon' do with it," Boogie started. "You won't know if I'm ready or right for the job until you put me in the position. I'm gon' let y'all know right now that I'm not my father. I'm me, and I'm gon' do things my way. If any of you thought that you were gon' vote my father's legacy, my legacy, to someone else, you were wrong. This seat is mine regardless of what you vote."

"How do you figure that?" Marco scoffed.

"Because my father left everything to me, including the businesses you wash some of your money through. All of you. Yeah, you could find other businesses who will clean your money, but that's a risk. A risk that would be silly to take when all you have to do is let a nigga sit down."

The room grew quiet when he was done speaking. Boogie watched them turn and look back and forth among each other. He could tell that they were shocked by the turn of events. He hadn't planned on saying all of that, but things had changed ever since he'd killed Shane. He wasn't the same person anymore. He hadn't grown coldhearted, but he refused to allow anyone else to reshape a destiny that had already been formed for him. Slowly, the four of them at the table began nodding their heads one by one.

"I think we all can agree that you definitely need some more grooming," Diana said, giving him a small smile, "but I think it's a unanimous decision. Sit down, Boogie."

She gestured an open palm to the seat. Boogie looked down at the chair, and although it was just a chair, it held so much importance. He rolled the executive chair out from underneath the table and sat down. He was officially the youngest head of the Five Families. He felt a warm sensation on his face and glanced over the table toward Caesar. Sure enough, he was watching him like a hawk. Boogie gave him his best smile and turned to Diana, who had just started the meeting.

Later that evening, Boogie pulled up to a nice one-story home in Brooklyn. The neighborhood was quiet, and Boogie smiled when he saw the little Honda in the driveway. With Shane out of the way, Bentley felt that it was time to get himself and his sister a place of their own. And now that he had some free time on his hands, Boogie felt that it was time to take Roz on the date he'd promised her.

He parked behind her in the driveway and got out. Before he reached the door, it swung open. Bentley was standing there holding baby Amber in his arms, but the moment she saw Boogie, she almost jumped out of them. During the time she and Roz had stayed with him, they'd grown accustomed to each other. He didn't think he had spent enough time with her for her to be so attached, but maybe she sensed that there was some goodness in him.

"What's poppin', baby girl?" he said and grabbed her before she fell to the ground with all of her fussing. "You missed me?"

She smiled up at him and patted his face with her chubby little hands. Her innocent face made his heart melt, and he knew right then that she would be able to get whatever she needed out of him.

"I see that I'ma have to teach her early," Bentley said, shaking her head. "She already got a thing for ugly niggas."

"You just mad that she likes me more than you, fool!" Boogie laughed and entered the home.

The two men slapped hands, and Bentley led him to the living room. Bentley had outdone himself with his home. He had a gray and white color scheme going on, and everything inside had been babyproofed. They sat down on the couch, and Boogie placed Amber on the floor. She was a fast little thing. As soon as her knees were planted, she crawled away to one of her toys that she spotted on the area rug.

"So, what happened today?" Bentley asked, literally on the edge of his seat. "You in or what?"

"What you think?" Boogie asked with a grin.

"Hell yeah! More money, here we come." Bentley rubbed his hands together. "Did you get a chance to holler at Marco for Gino?"

"Yeah. He said to have him come to the doc Saturday morning so he can check him out."

"A'ight, coo'. I'll tell him," Bentley said, and then his expression grew serious.

"You straight over there?" Boogie asked, noticing the drastic shift in his mood.

"Yeah. I was just wonderin' if you talked to Tazz, that's all."

"Nah, he good?"

"When he came over yesterday, he was good. He had some interesting shit to say about your uncle though."

"Who, Julius?"

"Yup. He said he kept meanin' to bring it up to you, but shit been so crazy lately."

"What about Julius?"

"I don't know. Somethin' about him actin' weird at your pops' funeral."

"His funeral? That was a minute ago," Boogie said, making a face.

"I know. Didn't you just hear me say he's been meanin' to bring it up to you?"

"Nigga . . ."

"A'ight, chill. My bad. But for real, he said that nigga was actin' real suspicious. And Tazz said he asked about the hit on Shane's condo. Did you know he knew about that?"

"Nah." Boogie shrugged. "But he could have easily found out about it."

"I don't know. He said he asked specifically if you had anything to do with it. Tazz always knew. He was in charge of the cleanup. He recognized A-Rod and Kirk off rip. But he didn't tell Julius that."

"What am I supposed to do with this information?" Boogie said, slightly amused. "He was in charge at the

time. He probably was just crossin' his t's and dottin' his
i's."

"Hopefully. You don't . . . you don't think he would have
had anything to do with Barry's murder, do you?"

"Unc?" Boogie had a look of disbelief on his face. "Hell
nah. My pop was like a father to him too. He wouldn't do
any snake shit like that."

"I don't know." Bentley hadn't been won over. "I think
you should go have a talk with him. Especially since
you're the head honcho in town. Make sure he under-
stands that."

Boogie opened his mouth to say something else, but
at that moment Roz came from the back room. Her face
was beaten with a flawless makeup look, and she wore
an off-shoulder cream sweater dress. Around her waist
was a thin Gucci belt that matched the brown thigh-high
heeled boots on her feet. Her hair was freshly straight-
ened, and the smile on her face matched Boogie's.

"You look nice," she told him. "I love the turtleneck
look on men."

"Thank you," he said, standing. "You ready to go?"

"Yes, let me just grab my clutch." She rushed back to
her bedroom to grab the small brown bag. When she got
back to the living room, she went to pick Amber up and
give her kisses. "Bentley, she needs to go to sleep in an
hour."

"A'ight," Bentley said when Roz handed Amber to him.

"I'm serious! The last time you babysat for me, you had
my baby up until one o'clock."

"Why she worried about what we do?" Bentley asked
Amber, who just smiled at him. "Tell her you have fun
with Uncle, huh? Tell her to take her fast ass on her date
and leave us alone."

"I'ma kick your ass," she said, and Boogie grabbed her by the hand before she could hit her brother upside the head.

"Come on, let's go. Our reservation is for eight thirty," he told her.

"Mm-hmm. Of course you save your little friend," she said and shot daggers at Bentley before they left.

He walked her to the passenger side of his vehicle and held the door open for her. He wanted to be chivalrous, but he also wanted to see her face light up the way it did when she saw the bouquet of roses on her seat. She picked them up and smelled them before turning toward Boogie.

"Thank you," she said.

"You're welcome, shorty. I left them in the car as a joke because I just knew you were gon' say somethin' about me not havin' them when I got in the house. I'm surprised you didn't."

"Boogie, I'm just happy I finally get some alone time with you," she said earnestly.

Before he could say anything else, she leaned into him and kissed him with a mixture of passion and longing. Their tongues entangled like they'd known each other before. It was a while before either of them came up for breath.

"I just wanted to get that out of the way," she whispered with her lips still so close to his that he could smell the mint on her breath. "Honestly, we can skip the date and go straight to your place. I've been wanting you so bad. And you're so good with Amber, and I'm around you all the time anyway. I know you're a nigga I can fuck with, Boogie. You don't have to do shit to impress me. I just want to skip all of this. I want to feel you inside of me over and over again."

Her words were like music to his ears, especially with everything he'd gone through lately. Having a shorty to come home to and help relieve his stress sounded good to him. Especially if it were her. He was tempted to take her up on her offer and skip the date, but he told his dick to shut up.

"Roz, I wanna date you proper, shorty," he breathed. "I know I've been havin' a lot of shit on my mind lately, but you're there too. You and Amber. Understand that. And I'm not gon' cap like I don't want the pussy. Lord knows I do. But I'm tryin'a fall in love with your mind, too. 'Cause I know I'm gon' love what's in between them thighs."

"Okay," she said and kissed his lips softly. "I'm with that."

"Good. Now come on. We can still make our reservation."

And they did. The restaurant Boogie had chosen to eat at was a steakhouse called Medallion. He'd gotten them a private section because he didn't want any distractions. The light over their table had been dimmed, and he ordered them one of the restaurant's finest bottles of champagne.

"I've never heard of this restaurant," Roz said after their waiter took their orders. "It's so fancy."

"My pop used to bring me here." Boogie shrugged like it was no big deal. "If he hadn't, I wouldn't have known about it either."

"Yeah, right. You're used to the finer things. You would have made your way here eventually," she teased.

"Trust, you're gon' grow accustomed to these things soon, I promise," Boogie said.

"Mm-hmm," she said and tried to hide her smile by turning away from him and grabbing her phone out of her purse. "I need to make sure my brother is putting Amber to sleep. That girl is cranky as hell in the morning if she doesn't get a full night's rest."

"Girl, if you don't leave them alone . . ."

"No, because I'm the only one who has to deal with it." She sent a quick text before putting her phone away and giving him her attention again. She shrugged her shoulders and exhaled. "You know, I never thought I would be a single mother. I always had these big plans for myself when I was younger. I would have the husband, the big house, and then the kids. So, when I got pregnant, I thought my life was over. I had to drop out of community college to get a full-time job because back then Bentley wasn't really making any money."

"What about Amber's father?" Boogie asked, realizing that they'd never talked about him before.

"He was a sorry excuse for a man while he was here."

"He moved?"

"No. He died in a car accident before she was even born. But either way, he didn't want anything to do with me or the baby. I think sometimes that maybe it worked out for the best. Now she won't have to grow up with the disappointment of having a father who didn't love her."

"That's tough. But you're doin' the damn thing on your own. Like you said, maybe it worked out for the best," Boogie said and then looked seriously at her. "Why were you talkin' all that 'skip this, skip that' shit outside the house? Everything good?"

"Yes, I'm good. I just . . ."

"You just what?"

"I don't want to miss out on something good when it comes to you, I guess." When she spoke, her eyes were on the red velvet tablecloth and not on him.

Boogie cupped her chin and forced her to give him eye contact. "Look at me when you speak your truth, shorty," he said, and she sighed.

Boogie had never seen Roz's vulnerable side, and he could tell she wasn't used to being that way. She was uncomfortable. Still, when it came to him, the only way was through.

"Boogie, seeing you handle your business just does something to me. And the shit you did for me and my brother, you didn't have to do that. But you did. You're a good man, Boogie. I've never met a man like you. Maybe I don't want to skip and rush things, but I'm definitely crushing hard. Normally men don't have me wide open like this. I feel stupid saying all this because I know you can have any woman you want. And who am I?"

"You're the woman I want," he said, taking her hand in his.

"For real? It's not just the champagne talking?"

"Stop playin' with me. I'm serious. Not even on any corny-nigga time. I fuck with you. With everything that's happened over the past month, not once did you trip or panic. That shit is sexy. You're thorough and I need that. Plus, I like that you like me for me. Since the first day I saw you, you did somethin' to my chest. I don't wanna call it love. It's too soon for all that. But if it goes that route, so be it. We can go as fast or slow as you want. But I just want you to know that you don't have to do nothin' to keep me. I'm here."

Roz blinked away the tears in her eyes and let out a happy laugh. "I feel like a simp bitch. Don't look at me," she said and dabbed her eyes.

Boogie had to laugh. The Roz he'd come to know was back. By the time their food came, they had finished half the bottle of champagne and were talking and laughing nonstop. The chemistry between them flowed so naturally, their souls might have known each other in another lifetime. He hadn't felt that happy in a while. Still, there was an underlying thought on his brain. He couldn't help but to ponder Bentley's choice words about Julius. It was strange that he had asked Tazz about something he didn't even mention to Boogie. But then again, if Tazz didn't say who was behind the hit, why would Julius have brought it up at all? Either way, Bentley was right about one thing.

After he and Roz finished eating, Boogie excused himself to the bathroom. He exited the dining floor and walked down a long hallway lined with dimly lit lamps. He waited for a few patrons to pass him before removing his phone from his pocket. He dialed Julius's number and waited for him to pick up.

"Nephew. To what do I owe this pleasure?" he said in a pleasant tone when he answered.

"What's good, Unc? We need to set up a meeting tomorrow to talk business," Boogie told him.

"Tomorrow? I won't have time."

"Make time," Boogie barked.

It felt a little strange being the one to call the shots. But there was no point going into his new position timid. He could tell that Julius hadn't expected that response because he grew quiet for a split second.

"When?" he finally asked.

"Seven o'clock. At Big Wheel."

"I'll see you tomorrow then. Love you, kid."

"Love you too."

They both disconnected the call. He let out a breath and shook the doubtful thoughts out of his head. Julius wasn't his enemy, and the last thing he wanted to do was make him feel like it. He told himself to ease up and went into the men's room to relieve himself. When he was done, there was a bathroom attendant inside who handed him a fresh towel to dry his hands on. Before Boogie left to rejoin his date, he tipped the man handsomely. Roz was already waiting by the door when he returned.

"I hope you washed your hands," Roz said, making a face. "You can't be holding my hand with piss on yours."

"Who said I wanted to hold your hand in the first place?" he teased.

"Oop," she said and opened her mouth in pretend shock. "It's like that?"

"Nah, girl. Come here."

He grabbed her hand and pulled her close to him as they walked out of the restaurant. For the first time that whole evening they were silent, but it was a silence that spoke volumes. They were full off each other's vibes, and it felt good for Boogie to just exist in the moment. He held her door open for her, and before she got in, she stroked his cheek tenderly. It was a simple gesture, but it was one that seemed to make all the pain Boogie had endured in the recent events of his life fade a little.

Chapter 16

A dark cloud hovered over Caesar as his driver slowed to a stop and parked by a curb. Caesar peered out of the back seat of the Rolls-Royce at an old, run-down building. It was a wet and cold day outside, as it had just rained, and Caesar spotted a few rats scurrying in front of it. The building had once been an old butchery in Staten Island years ago, and Caesar remembered going there a few times with his mother when it was open.

Two trucks pulled up to park behind him, and Caesar waited for his shooters to get out and scope out the surroundings. When they deemed it safe for him to step out of the vehicle, he did. He wore a jet-black Brunello Cucinelli single-breasted suit and had a mink thrown over his shoulders. Five men circled him, and one held an umbrella over his head as they led him to the entrance of the building. The others hung back. Manning the metal front door was a stocky Italian man wearing a navy blue suit and smoking a cigarette.

"You gentlemen must be lost," he said, flashing his gun.

Caesar didn't even glance at the pistol. What the man wasn't expecting was Caesar's impatience. He was the only thing in the way of Caesar getting to where he was going. "Move," he demanded.

"You must be out of your—"

He wasn't able to finish his sentence because Caesar's fist had plunged into his windpipe, crushing it. He fell to the ground holding his neck and gasping for air. Without medical attention he would surely die soon, but why wait? Caesar pulled out his Glock 19 pistol and slowly screwed the silencer on it. The man on the ground tried to scoot away, but Caesar's trigger finger was faster. The bullet left a neat circle in his temple, and his body went limp instantly. Caesar turned his head to the men still beside the cars and gave a single nod. They already knew what that meant. Popping the trunk to the SUV, they pulled out five AK-47 assault rifles, one for each of them. The men with him drew their pistols, and they all entered the building, ready for war.

After his cousin Douglas had brought him the photos revealing Bosco leaving Big Wheel shortly after the time of Barry's murder, Caesar had been on a search for him. Bosco was as slimy as an earthworm though. If he didn't want to be found, he went way underground. It had taken a while for Caesar to find Bosco's hideout, but once again with Douglas's intel, he finally figured out where it was. The building had been purchased under the name Rosa Bianchi a few years prior, and that also happened to be the name of Bosco's wife. It wasn't hard for Caesar to put two and two together. He didn't know why Bosco had targeted Barry, but he was about to find out what the consequence was.

The inside of the old butchery still smelled like raw meat. If over the years Caesar hadn't grown so accustomed to the smell of dead bodies, he would have gagged. Cautiously, they walked to the back where a freezer should have been, but instead they came upon a stairwell. It led them down to a concrete tunnel. Caesar made sure he had coverage to his front and back as they slowly walked down it toward the door.

Something didn't feel right. There were cameras everywhere, and Caesar had been prepared for an all-out gun war to ensue. The tunnel took them to a horizontal hallway, and at the end of it was another thick-looking metal door. That time, though, nobody was standing outside of it. He nodded for one of his shooters to open the door, and when they walked in, the lights suddenly came on. Caesar realized then why they hadn't been stormed by Italians. They had been waiting for them.

Standing in the center of what looked to be a miniature club was Bosco, puffing a cigar, and surrounding him was his own personal mob pointing guns at them. They were matched up body for body, and Caesar surveyed the room wearing a bored expression before stopping his eyes on the godfather wannabe.

"I knew you'd show up sooner or later. You aren't the only one with people in high places," Bosco stated. "And poor Marco. I saw how you shot him in the head. What am I going to tell his mother?"

"The same thing your wife will have to tell yours," Caesar suggested, and Bosco laughed.

"Caesar, Caesar, Caesar. It didn't have to be this way, you know. We could have been partners."

"We almost were," Caesar conceded. "But I'm glad it never happened. Did you think I wouldn't find out what you did to Barry?"

"And what exactly did I do to him?" Bosco asked, giving Caesar a slick smile.

"You know what you did." Caesar used that moment to pull out a photo taken by a camera outside Big Wheel. He tossed it to the red carpet next to Bosco's brown Kiton loafers.

Bosco glanced down at the photo and gave a loud laugh. "What is this?"

"A photo of you leaving the place Barry was murdered shortly after it happened."

"And?"

"And I know you were the one behind it. Be a man. Admit it so I can administer your punishment."

"See, that's where you're wrong," Bosco told him. "Was I there that night? Yes. But I showed up after he was already dead. I wasn't the one who took his life. Now inadvertently, yes, I may hold a little responsibility. I needed him out of the picture."

"Why?"

"Come on, Caesar. Think. You aren't that old yet. Why else? I want Brooklyn. And the Bronx, and Queens, and Harlem, and even Manhattan. And in order to get them, I needed somebody at your table. But you fucked that up by giving the kid a seat instead of—"

"Julius," Caesar finished for him. He could have shot himself in the foot for being so careless. Of course it was Julius. Caesar had spent so much time trying to find a mole in his own camp that he had neglected to thoroughly check Barry's. Maybe his old age was wearing him down. In his younger days, Caesar would have sniffed Julius out before things had even gotten that far.

Bosco took pleasure in Caesar's look of disbelief. "It took some time and planning, but eventually it happened. First, he got into bed with Shamar and Shane. Then he found me. Julius was to kill Barry, take his seat, and then we would kill you all off from the inside. He loved the plan, especially since he thought we were going to let him live once we got what we wanted. But you just had to be honorable and replace Barry with his son. Boogie, I think his name is. Hey, didn't Barry make you his godfather?" Bosco asked and was met with an icy gaze in response. He shrugged his shoulders and checked the diamond watch on his wrist. "I thought you'd just like to know that soon, in about an hour, he'll be joining his father in the graveyard."

"If you touch him, I'll—"

"Me? Why is it you keep assuming that it's me who does all this killing?" Bosco asked him, pretending to be hurt. "Save that little speech for Julius. Your godson doesn't even know what he's walking into. You're really losing your touch, old friend. You should have seen this coming. Did you think I would be good with this bullshit arrangement forever?"

"Bosco," Caesar said, gripping his gun in his hand tightly, "forgive me for my incompetence, but am I to believe that the only reason you're telling me all of this is because you aren't expecting me to walk out of here alive?"

"You know the answer to that already."

The two men locked eyes for an instant before each of them drew on each other and began firing at will. Caesar's mink went flying as he leapt to the side, shooting, and Bosco stepped behind one of his shooters to use him as a shield. Soon, everyone in the room was shooting, and debris was flying everywhere. Caesar's men held it down, and Bosco's men were dropping like flies. Caesar had landed behind a leather chair, and he used it for cover as he scanned the room for Bosco. It was hard to see with all of the dust flying around, but finally Caesar spotted him running through a beaded curtain that led somewhere else.

"Cover me!" he shouted before getting up and running after Bosco.

Caesar hit the beads out of his way as he cut into the hallway. There were a few rooms down that hallway, and Caesar kicked each of their doors in with his gun aimed and ready to shoot. When he finally reached the one at the end of the hall, he noticed the door on the right was already open. He went to peer inside of it but jumped back when bullets began flying his way. He ducked down low until he heard the clicking of the gun, letting him know that Bosco's clip was empty.

"Bosco, give it up," Caesar said, creeping into the room. "I'm gonna kill—"

"Aghh!" Bosco shouted as he came from out of nowhere.

He grabbed Caesar's wrist and wrestled him for his weapon. The surprise attack gave Bosco an advantage, and he made Caesar drop his gun. When he made a grab for it, Caesar kicked it so it slid across the carpet, and he knocked Bosco back into the wall. He went to punch him again, but Bosco ducked out of the way, grabbed Caesar by the waist, and wrestled him to the floor. Soon his hands were wrapped around Caesar's neck, and he tried to choke him out. As he gasped for air, Caesar reached toward his ankle and pulled a small revolver from it. He pointed it at Bosco's gut and fired twice. The evil expression he had been looking down at Caesar with quickly turned into one of shock. His grip loosened, and he looked at the two red dots on the white shirt underneath his suit jacket. Caesar pushed him to the ground and stood back up.

"You fucked up, Bosco," he said before placing a bullet right between the Italian's eyes.

He grabbed his gun off the floor and tucked it in his waist. He noticed that he no longer heard gunfire coming from the front, and he didn't know if that was a good thing or a bad thing. He crept back down the hallway holding his gun in both hands and preparing to shoot anything walking. But when he got to the front, he saw the reason it was so quiet.

Everyone was dead, including all the men he'd come with. The blood seeping from the bodies made dark, wet spots on the already-red carpet. Still, he wouldn't let down his guard until he was sure all of the Italians were done for. Suddenly, he heard a noise coming from the entrance. When he looked up, he saw a man standing in the doorway looking around at the gory scene. He was openly taken aback, and Caesar recognized him as none other than Shamar Hafford. They'd never met personally, but Caesar knew what he looked like from pictures. Briefly, the two kingpins looked at each other before Caesar started shooting in his direction. The bullets ricochet off the metal door, and Shamar turned and ran in the opposite direction.

Caesar started to run after him, but then he remembered the danger Boogie was in. He grabbed his phone and tried to call and warn him, but he kept getting sent to voicemail. He didn't know what Boogie's recent problem with him was, but it was apparent that the two had something to hash out. He tried to call again, but he was sent to voicemail once more.

"What the hell is wrong with this kid!" Caesar exclaimed.

He ran as quickly as his aching body would take him back outside to where his car was parked. When he was outside, he looked up and down the sidewalk to see if Shamar was somewhere hiding before getting into the back seat of the Rolls-Royce.

"Clarence, take me to Big Wheel in Brooklyn as fast as you can! It's important," he instructed. When Clarence didn't budge, Caesar shook the middle-aged man's shoulder. "Clarence!"

Clarence's head rolled to the side and revealed that he had a huge hole in the side of his head. He was dead. Shamar must have killed him on the way inside.

Caesar got back out of the vehicle and pulled Clarence's body from the driver seat and onto the street pavement. He then got behind the wheel himself, not caring that there was fresh blood on his seat. Starting the car, he peeled off from the curb in the direction of Big Wheel Automotive.

"Hold on, Boogie, I'm coming."

Chapter 17

Caesar tried to remember the last time his heart had beat to the point where he thought it was going to explode out of his chest. Maybe before his daughter was born, and maybe again when her mother left her on his doorstep to raise alone. Either way, both times were long ago. But right then, he was just praying that he wouldn't see Boogie sprawled out in a pool of his own blood when he walked into Big Wheel.

He turned the Rolls-Royce into the vacant parking lot and looked at the building. All of the lights in the building were on, but he didn't see anybody inside. Still, he knew Julius was there somewhere. He reloaded his Glock and put his revolver in the armrest before hopping out of the car. He burst inside the building and decided against going to find Julius. Instead, he stood right by the front counter. He wouldn't give another person the upper hand on him that night.

"Why don't you come on out, Julius? I know everything. There's no point playing games with me."

At first there was silence, but then Caesar heard the sound of clapping getting closer and closer until finally Julius materialized from the back. He was dressed in a black hoodie, a pair of jeans, and a pair of Timberland boots. He clapped a few more times and then stopped abruptly.

"So, you finally figured it out, huh?"

Caesar wanted to shoot the stupid smile off his face. However, he had some questions that he needed answered. "Why, Julius? Barry was good to you. He treated you like a son."

"No, he treated me like a charity case," Julius said. "He put me in a position that he wanted me content in for the rest of my life. You know, all those years he thought I was just a great white, but I'm a megalodon, baby. And I don't swim well with other sharks. I needed him out of the way. And Bosco, Shamar, and even Shane helped me achieve that."

"You stupid-ass boy. Bosco was just going to kill you after he was done with you. Don't you know that?"

"I was going to be sure that I got him first."

"Too late. I beat you to the punch," Caesar told him. "Before I put a bullet in his head, he told me about your plan. Disloyalty is repaid with death. Don't you know that?"

"If that's the case, why is Barry dead?" Julius asked with a laugh. "He'd started to catch on to me, you know. It was right after he changed his will that I just noticed him acting different toward me. And then that night, he called me here to Big Wheel. . . ."

As Barry walked into Big Wheel, his phone was ringing off the hook. He checked the screen and saw that it was Marco calling again. Barry was supposed to head back to Queens that night to drop off a payment for some new automatic handguns, but first he had something to take care of. All of his employees had gone home for the day, which was fine, because they didn't need to witness what was about to take place.

He'd asked Julius to meet him there that evening because they had some things they needed to discuss. Barry didn't want him to think that anything was wrong, which was the only reason he hadn't walked in there mobbed up, but he was furious. He'd recently found out that there was a rat in his camp, and before he did anything about it, he wanted to look in the rat's face and ask why. Anybody else would have been dead the instant he found out some news like that, but Julius had been like a son to him. He wanted to give him the benefit of the doubt. He didn't want to believe that he had been feeding the Italians information about their business dealings, but his source said otherwise.

Quiet as kept, Barry had been having Julius followed the last few weeks because something about the way he was moving didn't sit right with Barry. Some of the things he said raised a red flag. Barry had been sure it was just his paranoia, but as usual, his gut instinct seemed to be right. Julius was seen frequently coming and going to Staten Island, a place they had no business being.

He walked back toward his office to wait for Julius to get there, but he was surprised to see that he was already there dressed in black. In fact, he was sitting in Barry's seat with his feet kicked up.

"What do you think you're doing?" Barry asked, referring to Julius's disrespect.

"What does it look like I'm doing?" Julius said and then waved his hand around the room. "I'm getting used to my new desk."

"So it's true, then." Barry shook his head. "Dammit, Julius! What the fuck is wrong with you? Why would you get into bed with the Italians?"

"Because they offered me a way better deal than you."

"I take care of you. I keep you fed."

"See, that's the problem right there. If you allow someone to feed you, then you can also allow them to starve you. I don't want to be fed anymore. I want to be the boss."

"Well, that job is already taken. How did you know what I was going to do here tonight?" Barry asked.

"I bugged your office. That's how I found out you were having me tailed." Julius laughed. "And after tonight, your position will be open."

"You would go against the Pact?" Barry asked, and Julius acted like he was scared.

"Oh, no, the Pact. Whatever shall I do?" Julius's voice dripped in sarcasm. "Nigga, do you think I give a fuck about that little Pact y'all got? When I'm done doing what I have to do, there won't even be Five Families left to have a Pact. You know the funniest thing?"

"What?" Barry asked.

"You really thought you were going to come in here and kill me." Julius snickered like someone had just told a joke, and then he snapped his fingers.

Barry reached for his gun, but he wasn't quick enough. Footsteps coming up behind him caught him off guard. He didn't even have time to turn around. He felt something hard bludgeon him in the back of his head, and then everything went black.

Caesar didn't know which made his stomach turn more: hearing the story of how Barry had been caught slacking, or the sick Cheshire cat grin on Julius's face. He now understood why a while ago Diana said that Barry had seemed on edge. He knew his right-hand man was a snake. Caesar just wished he'd come to them for help. He might still be alive.

"Technically, me killing him was self-defense. It was either him or me, and well, you know the rules of the jungle."

"Shut the fuck up. Where is Boogie?"

"First you bust in here interrupting my conversation with the love of my life. Now you're asking stupid questions. Well, Caesar, your age is showing, because you're actually early to the party." Julius quickly pursed his lips and turned his palms up. "Oh, there he is right now."

He pointed toward the outside of the building, and Caesar foolishly turned his head. There was nobody in the parking lot. The only thing he saw was his own car. When he turned back around, Julius was leaping for his gun. Knowing that his old body couldn't take another physical showdown, Caesar squeezed the trigger relentlessly. Each bullet that hit Julius's body made him take a step backward. The close range of the bullets hitting him in the chest made blood pour from his lips.

"F . . . fuck." Julius tried to reach for the counter to hold himself up, but he was too weak.

"This is for Barry," Caesar said and fired one last bullet into his body.

Julius hit the wall behind him, and his eyes rolled back as he slid to the floor. Caesar let the hand holding his gun fall to his side. He breathed heavily knowing that now the only person he had to get rid of was Shamar. He doubted that he was going to stay in New York for long if he hadn't already left. *No matter*. Caesar vowed to get him one way or another.

Chapter 18

Boogie checked the time in his car and saw that he was running a little late that evening. He had told Julius that he would be there by seven, but here it was pushing seven thirty. He'd been kicking it with Roz and had lost track of time. Hopefully Julius was still there, because he hadn't called and asked him where Boogie was yet.

Boogie just hoped that it would be a smooth transition. He had never had to take order or direction from somebody younger than him, but he hoped Julius would be open to being his counsel. Because things were how they were, and they weren't going to change. Boogie wanted business to go on as usual, because now it was on him to not only make sure the underground game was good, but the businesses above ground as well. Boogie noticed that the cleaners hadn't been repaired or remodeled after the shooting, and also the second location of Big Wheel wasn't finished. He wanted to know exactly what Julius had handled while he was temporarily in charge.

When he finally pulled into the parking lot of the auto shop, the first thing he saw was Caesar's Rolls-Royce. However, he didn't see Julius's BMW anywhere. It must have been parked out back. He wondered why Caesar was there. He was the last person Boogie wanted to see. While he'd been with Roz, Caesar had called him multiple times, but Boogie wasn't trying to talk. Just saying his name was enough to make Boogie have a bad taste in his mouth. Once he parked, he got out and went inside, planning to avoid Caesar.

"Juli—" Boogie started to yell, but he stopped in the middle of saying his uncle's name.

What he saw was enough to make his jaw drop slightly. Caesar was standing by the front counter holding a smoking gun. On the ground in front of him was Julius. He was in a sitting position with his back against the wall, and it wasn't hard to tell that he was dead. Julius was dead.

"What the fuck did you do?" he asked, horrified. "Caesar, what the fuck did you do?"

"Boogie . . ."

When Caesar turned toward him with the gun still in his hand, Boogie pulled out his own fire and pointed it at him. The sight of the gun didn't seem to intimidate Caesar, because he tried to take a step toward him.

"Stay the fuck away from me!" Boogie breathed. "You killed him. You killed Unc! Just like you did my pop."

"Boogie, no."

"I knew it. Why?"

"I had to. He was doing business with the Italians."

"Yeah, right," Boogie scoffed. "That was you who tried that, remember?"

"That was a long time ago, Boogie."

"You're lyin'! You probably killed my pop and Julius to get them out of the way so you could finally do what you've always wanted to. My mama said I shouldn't trust you."

"Boogie, you have it all wrong."

"Yeah? Then why didn't you ever tell me you were my godfather? Huh? Where the fuck were you my whole life? But as soon as my dad is dead, you wanna take me under your wing and shit. Nigga, I should kill you!"

He couldn't stop the tears from coming to his eyes. He had been right the whole time. He didn't know the impact the truth would have on him. He didn't think he would be so affected. He had lost his father, Julius, and now Caesar.

He aimed his gun at Caesar's chest and put his finger on the trigger. His mind screamed for him to do it, to shoot Caesar right in the heart and bleed him out, because that was where he was aching the most. But he just couldn't bring himself to do it. He let the gun fall to his side in his hand and steadied his shaky breath.

"I'm done," he said, staring into the pained expression on Caesar's face. "I'm out. Brooklyn is out. From now on, you and the others need to stay the fuck out of my territory or I'll kill you. I'll kill you all."

He turned his back and left the auto shop before he could change his mind.

Chapter 19

It was hard watching Boogie walk away from him, but Caesar knew he had to. He wasn't trying to hear what Caesar was trying to tell him. He thought they were all lies, so there was no point in telling him that his life had just been saved. Now Boogie's mood change toward him made sense to Caesar finally. He recognized the rage in his godson. It reminded him of when he found out his mother died. He wanted the entire world to pay, and he had to learn on his own that he couldn't have that. One day, Boogie would know the truth, but it was up to him to want it. Still, Caesar had to force himself to go after the boy. He was fearful of the hurt he would put on the world with all that anger inside of him.

Caesar took another look at Julius. He'd caused so much hurt and pain in the ones who loved him when they didn't have to. Caesar couldn't understand what could possess a person to turn on those kinds of people There wasn't enough money or power in the world that could replace the love of family. Because, yes, if he had succeeded, he would have been on top. But he would have been all alone. Eventually he would have learned that, and when he did, he would have spent the rest of his life trying to undo all of his wrongs. Caesar learned the hard way.

Julius's blood had started to spread throughout the business, and Caesar knew it needed to be cleaned up right away. He went for his phone to call a cleaner team and have them come out that night. Right when he was about to press the green call button, he heard a rustling sound coming from the back. He exited what he was doing on the phone and put it back in his pocket. He had thought he and Julius had been the only ones there before Boogie had come and gone, but maybe he was wrong. Suddenly, he heard footsteps coming down the hallway from the back offices, and Caesar aimed his gun, preparing to shoot. When the person stepped out of the hallway shadow and into the light, Caesar's forehead crinkled in confusion.

"Dina?"

Dina Tolliver stared at Caesar's muddled expression with a hateful look of her own. He couldn't understand why she had been there with Julius. She didn't say a word. Instead she knelt down beside Julius's dead body. She grabbed his lifeless hand and kissed his knuckles before bowing her head. The entire scenario didn't make any sense to Caesar, but then he thought back to something that Julius had said.

"First you bust in here interrupting my conversation with the love of my life."

"No." Caesar didn't want to believe it. "Dina. You and Julius?"

"That's right," she said, wiping her eyes. She stared fondly at Julius before placing his hand down gently and standing up. "He was the love of my life."

"But you were married to Barry."

"And do you think being married to me stopped that man from frequenting the Sugar Trap? I lost count of how many times he came home smelling like liquor and cheap perfume. He stopped being the man I married years ago, and I stopped trying to force it out of him."

"So, you had an affair with Julius? Of all people?"

"Yes, I did," Dina said smugly. "And it was the best decision I ever made in my life. He didn't care about the age difference between us. He loved me just the same. When he told me about his plan to kill Barry—"

"You knew?" he asked in disbelief.

"Of course I knew," she said to him as if he were stupid. "And I was all for having that bastard out of my life forever. And when I found out about that new will from my lawyer when Barry died, I tried to get rid of all of Barry's assets before Boogie found out. But somehow, that cheap, pussy-chasing son of a bitch still was able to reach out from the grave. He left everything to Boogie. Everything. Like I wasn't the one who helped him build it! And from the ground up, too."

Caesar got over his shock and took into account that Dina was wearing all black. Not only that, but it was a known fact that Julius had been there to kill Boogie. And if she was there, she had to have known that too.

"Dina, were you planning to help Julius murder your own son?"

Dina stared at Caesar, and for a while her eyes seemed to go somewhere else. She'd changed and not for the better. Slowly, a smile ran across her face, and she returned to the moment.

"Do you know how hard it is to fake tears at a funeral?" she asked, still wearing the same loopy smile. "I had to keep going to the bathroom and applying drops. My eyes burned for days after that, but it was worth it. Boogie really thought I was broken up about it." She paused to give a breathy laugh. "Can you believe that? I love my son. I really do. But he always belonged to his father. Even when Barry turned his back on him, and I was the one who told that man not to be so hard on the boy. I wanted him to go and live his chef dream. I didn't want him even thinking about taking Barry's place once he was out of the way, so Julius and I could live the life Barry should have given me. But no, he wanted to come back and ruin my plans. He couldn't just go on and live his life. Why? Why couldn't he have just left?"

Dina's smile left her face, and she began to sob uncontrollably. Her shoulders shook violently as the tears rolled down her face. But just as quickly as she started crying, she stopped. Caesar knew then that she was very unstable. It wasn't the first time he'd seen a woman in her position. Crimes of passion very seldom had good rewards in the end.

"Julius was a manipulator and a liar," Caesar told her. "He was just using you. Once he got what he wanted from you, he would have dropped you. Or worse, killed you because you knew too much."

"No! Don't say that. Don't you dare say that! Before you came, Julius and I had the most beautiful conversation about how once Boogie was out of the way for good, we were going to go on vacation in Hawaii for two weeks. Do you know how long it's been since somebody took me on vacation? Or wanted to do anything nice for me? I needed that. I needed him."

"He got you on board with the death of your husband, and tonight, you would have killed your own son for him. Boogie doesn't deserve that!"

"You're saying that like the boy even likes you right now. I heard the little exchange between the two of you. He is pretty pissed at you, isn't he? I heard him say he doesn't want any part of you and the cool club anymore. That's gotta hurt, huh? Bet you wish now you'd had a relationship with him."

"I do," Caesar admitted. "But it isn't too late for that. Just like it isn't too late for you. Let me get you help, Dina. You aren't right in the head."

"Help?" Dina scoffed. "I don't need help! All I need is my man. Did I tell you he's taking me to Hawaii?"

"Dina, he's dead."

"Dead?" she asked, confused, and then looked back at Julius. Her face dropped when her eyes landed on all the blood, but only for a split second. "Oh, that's right. He's dead. I almost forgot that I have to repay you for that."

From her pocket she brandished a Beretta and aimed it right at Caesar. It was like he was frozen in place when she pulled the trigger. When the bullet hit him in the chest, his life flashed before his eyes. She shot the gun again, that time hitting him in the stomach. She smiled gleefully as he staggered back until he finally fell to the ground.

"And you don't have to worry about me hurting Boogie now. My son is going to take care of his mama the way his daddy should have and the way Julius wanted to. He'll be happy to know you're dead. Goodbye, Caesar. I think I want to let you die alone."

She put the gun back in her pocket and stepped casually over his body. The door dinged when she opened it, and when it shut, he knew she was gone because it was quiet. The fiery pain in his chest was so painful that he couldn't catch his breath. The world around Caesar began to fade, and Caesar's last regret before he closed his eyes to succumb to the pain was that he had lived a life of so many regrets.